I0688018

John G. (John Gosse) Freeze

A Royal Pastoral

And other Poems

John G. (John Gosse) Freeze

A Royal Pastoral
And other Poems

ISBN/EAN: 9783337162948

Printed in Europe, USA, Canada, Australia, Japan

Cover: Foto ©Andreas Hilbeck / pixelio.de

More available books at **www.hansebooks.com**

A ROYAL PASTORAL

And Other Poems

BY

JOHN GOSSE FREEZE

———————

NEW YORK

E. & J. B. YOUNG & CO.

COOPER UNION, FOURTH AVENUE

1896

Copyright, 1896, by
JOHN G. FREEZE

One hundred copies only printed, of which this is No.............................

TABLE OF CONTENTS.

POEMS TO MARGARET.

ECCLESIASTES.

Invocation.

COME, beardless Leader of the Sacred Nine,
  Unshorn Apollo, from thy heavenly hill,
Once more to earth thine influence incline,
And burning thoughts into my mind instil.
Without thy kindly aid my voice must still
Raise scarce an echo the low vales among,
And like the purling of a puny rill
That hardly glads the mead it creeps along,
Without effect or force must flow my nameless song.

Resume again thy long forsaken seat,
Take up the sceptre thou wast wont to sway,
Touch my young lip with accents pure and sweet,
And grant me strength stern virtue to obey :
Turn not thine ear from my request away,
Vouchsafe me power to tune the Lyre Divine,
To calm the passions cheer, the weary way,
To pay to love the tributary line,
To leave a name on earth when I its cares resign.

A Royal Pastoral.

DRAMATIS PERSONÆ.

THE KING.	CHORUS OF YOUTHS.
THE BRIDE.	THE BRIDE'S BROTHERS.
CHORUS OF VIRGINS.	THE KING'S ATTENDANTS.

SCENE FIRST.

THE KING'S CHAMBERS.

CHORUS OF VIRGINS—THE BRIDE.

CHORUS OF VIRGINS.

LET him kiss me with the kisses of his
mouth.
Better thine endearments far, than
wine.
Sweet as is the fragrance of thy banquet,
Yet is thy name the best of all perfumes,
Sweeter than all fragrance wide diffused:
Thus are we drawn, thus do we follow thee,

Thus hath the King brought us to his chambers;
We will be happy and rejoice in thee;
Though we forget the wine of thy banquet,
Thy love sweeter far we still remember:
For uprightness do the virgins love thee.

THE BRIDE.

Ye daughters of Jerusalem!
  I am black but comely—
  As the tents of Kedar—
As the curtains of Solomon.

Scorn me not because of my blackness—
Because the sun hath looked upon me:
My mother's sons were jealous of me,
They made me keeper of the vineyards,
But mine own vineyard have I not kept.

Tell me, O thou whom my soul loveth,
Whither dost thou lead and feed thy flock?
Where dost thou make it to repose at noon?
For why should I be as one astray
  By the flocks of thy companions?

CHORUS OF VIRGINS.

If thou know not,
Thou fairest among women,
Go thy way forth
By the footsteps of the flock,
And feed thy kids
Beside the shepherds' tents.

The King enters.

THE KING.

Thou art likened, my Beloved,
To a company of horses
In the chariots of Pharaoh ;
Comely are thy cheeks with jewels,
And necklaces adorn thy neck.

CHORUS OF VIRGINS.

Chains of gold will we make thee,
And ornaments of silver
Set round with priceless jewels.

THE BRIDE.

While the King sitteth at his banquet,
My spikenard its fragrance sendeth forth ;

A bundle of myrrh is my Beloved,
In my arms shall he lie all the night :
My Love is a cluster of henna
From the vineyards of En-gedi.

THE KING.

Lo ! thou art beautiful,
Lo ! thou art fair, my Love,
Eyes hast thou like the dove.

THE BRIDE.

Lo ! thou too art fair, Beloved,
Yea, pleasant in all gladsome things :

Our couch is green and flourishing.

THE KING.

The beams of our house are of cedar,
The galleries are builded of the fir,
And the rafters thereof are of cypress.

THE BRIDE.

I am the rose of Sharon,
The lily of the valleys.

THE KING.

As the lily among the thorns,
Is my love among the daughters.

THE BRIDE.

As the apple-tree among the trees of the wood,
  Is my Love among the sons;
I sat down under his shadow with great delight,
  And his fruit was pleasant to my taste;
He brought me with him to the house of ban-
    queting,
  And his banner over me was love.

Sings:
Strengthen me with flagons,
Comfort me with apples,
For I am sick of love.

O that his left hand were under my head
And that his right hand did embrace me!

I adjure you! daughters of Jerusalem,
By the roes and by the hinds of the field,
That ye stir not up, nor waken my Love,
  Until he please.
End of Scene First.

SCENE SECOND.

THE BRIDE'S CHAMBER.

THE BRIDE, THE CHORUS OF VIRGINS.

Monologue to the Chorus.

THE BRIDE.

The sound of my Beloved !
Behold ! behold he cometh,
Leaping upon the mountains,
Skipping upon the hills :
   My Beloved cometh
   Like as a roe,
   Or a young hart.

Lo ! he standeth behind our wall,
He looketh in through the windows,
Shewing himself at the lattice ;
He speaketh unto me and saith :—

Rise, my friend, my beautiful !
   Arise and come away,

For lo! the winter is past,
The rain is over and gone,
The flowers appear on the earth,
The time for the pruning is come,
The voice of the turtle is heard,
The fig-tree is sweetening her fruit,
The vine blossom gives forth her smell ;
Rise, my Love, my beautiful !
    Arise and come away.
My dove in the clefts of the rocks,
Hiding among the steep places,
Thy countenance let me behold,
The voice of thy song let me hear,
For sweet is the voice of thy song,
Thy countenance comely to see.

Sings :

Catch us the foxes,
Catch the little foxes,
Wasting our vineyards
While they are tender—
While they are blossoming.

My Beloved is mine and I am his,
He feedeth among the lilies.

> Until the evening come—
> Until the shadows flee—
> Until the day breathe cool—
> Turn, My Beloved, turn ;
> And be thou like a roe,
> Or like to a young hart
> On the mountains that divide us.

By night on my bed I sought
Him whom my soul loveth ;
I sought him but I found him not.
Come, I said, let me rise now,
Let me go about the city,
In the streets and in the broadways
Seeking him whom my soul loveth :
I sought him but I found him not.

The watchmen that go about the city
Found me seeking him whom my soul loveth—
Saw ye him, I said, whom my soul loveth ?
But a little way had I passed from them
When I found him whom my soul loveth ;
I held him, and I would not let him go
Until I brought him to my mother's house,
Into her chamber that conceivèd me.

Daughters of Jerusalem !
By the roes and by the hinds
I charge ye,
Stir not up
Nor waken
My Love, until he please.
End of Scene Second.

SCENE THIRD.

THE ESPOUSALS.

CHORUS OF YOUTHS.

Describing the Wedding Procession.

First.

Who then is this ascending from the valleys,
Up from the wilderness wrapped in clouds of
    smoke,
Richly perfumed with myrrh and frankincense,
Fragrant with the spices of the merchant?

Second.

Behold—the royal couch of Solomon !
Three score men of valor are about it,

All men of might, all men expert in war,
Each with his sword girded upon his thigh,
Fearful of the frequent night alarum!

First.

King Solomon hath made himself a chariot,
A chariot of the wood of Lebanon ;
The pillars, its supports, are of silver,
And the canopy and covering are of gold ;
The seat is royal with a purple cushion.
The bottom wrought with goodly tapestry
By the fair daughters of Jerusalem.

All.

Come forth, O Zion's daughters, and behold
King Solomon, glad in his nuptial crown,
Wherewith his mother crowned him in the day
Of his espousals and his heart's great gladness.

THE KING.

Meeting the Procession.

Lo ! thou art beautiful, my Love,
All fair, my Love, all beautiful !

Thine eyes like dove's behind thy veil;
Thy hair is as a flock of goats
That couch upon Mount Gilead;
Thy teeth are like a flock of sheep
Coming up in pairs from washing;

Thy lips are like a scarlet thread,
And comely is thy fragrant mouth;
And like a piece of pomegranate
Thy cheeks appear behind thy veil.
Thy neck is like King David's tower,
Well builded for an armory,
Whereon a thousand bucklers hang,
The well-known shields of mighty men.
Thy breasts are like two young twin roes
That feed among the lilies sweet.

THE BRIDE.

Until the eventide—
Until the shadows flee—
Unto the mount of myrrh,
The hill of frankincense,
O, let me hie!

End of Scene Third.

SCENE FOURTH.

THE PALACE GARDEN.

THE KING, THE BRIDE, ATTENDANTS.

THE KING.

Thou art all beautiful, my Love,
And fair—there is no spot in thee!

Come now with me from Lebanon,
With me from Lebanon, O Bride!
And with me shalt thou wander forth
From Amana, from high Shenir,
And look abroad from Hermon cool
On the darkening dens of lions,
On the mountain haunts of leopards.

O my sister, my bride!
Thou hast ravished my heart!
With one glance of thine eyes,
With one chain of thy neck,
Thou hast ravished my heart.

O how pleasant thy loves,
How much better than wine ;
The smell of thine unguents
Is sweeter than spices—
More grateful than spices,
Thy lips distil sweetness,
    My sister, my bride,
    For honey and milk
    Are under thy tongue.
The smell of thy garments
Is like Mount Lebanon.

And a garden enclosed
Is my sister, my bride,
And a spring walled up,
And a fountain sealed ;
A pomegranate orchard,
With trees of pleasant fruits—
The spikenard and henna,
The calamus and saffron,
The fragrant cinnamon,
With trees of frankincense,
The aloes and sweet myrrh,
And of all spices chief.

A garden of fountains,
A well of bright waters,
And streams from Lebanon.

THE BRIDE.

Awake, O north wind !
And come, thou south wind !
Blow upon my garden
And diffuse the fragrance
Of its spicery :
Let my Beloved come
Early to his garden,
And eat his pleasant fruits !

THE KING.

I have come to my garden,
My sister, my bride ;
I have gathered my myrrh,
I have gathered my spice,
And my honeycomb sweet
With my honey have eat,
And have drunken my wine
With my milk, O my bride !

To his Companions.

Eat, O friends—drink, yea, drink,
And fill yourselves with loves.

End of Scene Fourth.

SCENE FIFTH.

THE BRIDE'S CHAMBER—HER SECOND DREAM.

THE BRIDE, THE CHORUS OF VIRGINS.

Monologue to the Chorus.

THE BRIDE.

I sleep, but my heart waketh—
Hark! my Beloved knocketh—
"Open to me, my sister, my Bride,
My love, my dove, my undefiled,
For my head is filled with the dew,
My locks with the drops of the night."

"I have put off my coat,
How shall I put it on?

> I have washed my feet,
> How shall I defile them ?"

My Love put his hand to the door,
To him my desires were gone forth,
Then I rose up to open the door,
Then I put out my hands to the door,
They dropped with the freshest of myrrh,
My fingers with sweet-smelling myrrh,
Poured over the handles and bolt ;—
Then opened I to my Beloved,
But he had withdrawn and was gone ;
My soul had gone out as he spake ;
I sought him, he could not be found,
I called him, he answered me not.
The watchmen that go through the city,
They found me, and smote me, and hurt me ;—
They took away from me my veil,
Those watchmen upon the walls.

She Wakes.

Daughters of Jerusalem !
I charge you, if ye find
My friend—my Beloved—

This message ye shall bear,
" That I am sick of love."

CHORUS OF VIRGINS.

What is thy Beloved more than another,
  O fairest among women ;
What is thy Beloved more than another,
  That thou dost so adjure us ?

THE BRIDE.

My Beloved is white and ruddy,
Among ten thousand, he is chief,
His head is as the most fine gold,
His locks are as the waving palm,
His eyes are as the eyes of doves,
Set fitly by the water-streams ;
Like beds of spices are his cheeks,
Fair builded towers of sweet perfumes ;
His lips like scarlet lilies are,
Moist with the sweetly liquid myrrh ;
His hands as gold with beryl set,
His body bright as ivory,
With sapphire wrought and laden o'er ;
His legs as marble pillars are,

On golden sockets firmly set ;
His aspect, grand as Lebanon,
As its tall cedars excellent ;
His mouth bewitches every heart,
And to him are my fond desires.

This my Beloved—this my friend,
O daughters of Jerusalem !

THE CHORUS.

Whither is thy Beloved gone,
    O thou fairest among women !
Whither is he turned aside,
    That we may seek him with thee ?

THE BRIDE.

My Beloved has gone to his garden,
Among beds of sweet spices to wander,
To feed on the fruits of his garden,
To gather the sweet-smelling lilies ;
My Beloved is mine—I am his,
He feedeth among the sweet lilies.

Enter THE KING.

Thou art fair, my Love, as Tirzah,
Thou art comely as Jerusalem,
And glorious as a bannered host.—
Turn away thy bright eyes from me,
They consume me in their brightness ;
Thy hair is as a flock of goats
That couch upon Mount Gilead ;
Thy teeth are as a flock of sheep,
Coming up in pairs from washing,
Whereof each one beareth twins,
And no barren one among them ;
Like a piece of ripe pomegranate
Are thy cheeks behind thy veil.
Of married Queens threescore,
Of fourscore lawless loves,
Of virgins numberless,
One only is my dove—
My pure, my perfect one—
Her mother's loved one He—
The darling of her heart—
Thrice blest who gave her birth !
The daughters gazed on her,
And gazing called her blest ;

The Queens and lawless loves,
The virgins numberless,
While gazing sang her praise.

End of Scene Fifth.

SCENE SIXTH.

THE MORNING BREAKS—THE BRIDE COMES FORTH.

THE CHORUS.

Who then is this with glances like the dawn,
Fair as the silver moon,
Bright as the noonday sun,
And awe-inspiring as a bannered host ?

THE BRIDE.

One who went down into the walnut garden,
The coming fruits to see and blooming apple-
trees,
Watching the vine open its tender blossoms,
And the pomegranate-tree bursting into bud :
There was my soul awakened from its slumber—

There was my heart filled with the fire of love—
There unawares my virgin charms had set me
On the chariots of a people of renown.

THE CHORUS.

Return! return! O Shulamite, return!
Return, that we may look upon thee more!

THE BRIDE.

What will ye with the Shulamite?

THE CHORUS.

The sacred dance of Mahanaim.

She Dances.

THE CHORUS.

How dainty are thy sandal'd feet,
O daughter of a princely house!
Thy joints are set like jewels rare,
The cunning craftsman's handy work;
Thy girdle bears a moon-shaped bowl,
Where wine well mixed shall never fail;
Thy body is a heap of wheat

Covered and set with lilies sweet ;
Thy neck a tower of ivory ;
Thine eyes like Heshbon's sparkling pools,
Bath-Rabbim's gateways close beside ;
Thy brow like Lebanon's high tower,
Which toward Damascus looketh down ;
Thy stately head like Carmel's mount
Whose hair, with rich and purple tint,
A king within its tresses binds.

Enter THE KING.

How fair and what a charm hast thou,
O Love, amid delightsome things—
Thy stature like the stately palm,
Thy charms like clusters of the grape :
I will approach the stately palm,
I will embrace the boughs thereof ;
Thy charms like clustering grapes shall be,
Thy breath like apples breathing sweet
Thy mouth distil the best of wine.

THE BRIDE.

For my Beloved flowing sweetly,
Causing the lips that sleep to speak.

I belong to my Beloved,
His desire is ever towards me.

Come, my Beloved, hie we to the fields,
Let us lodge there in the villages—
Let us go up early to the vineyards—
Let us see if the vine flourishes,
If the vine blossom has yet opened,
And the pomegranate be in flower:—
There my caresses will I give to thee!
Now the mandrakes yield their spicy fragrance,
And at our house is every choicest fruit,
The new, the old, laid up in store for thee.
O that thou wert to me as my brother,
That reposed on the breast of my mother;
When I should find thee, then would I kiss thee,
Kiss thee without and none would despise me;
Then would I bring thee to my mother's house,
There shouldst thou teach me passionate caresses,
There drink spiced wine of the juice of my pome-
    granate.
                    To the Chorus.

Then should his left hand be under my head,
And then should his right hand embrace me.

I charge you, daughters of Jerusalem!
That ye stir not up, nor waken my Love,
Until he please.

End of Scene Sixth.

SCENE SEVENTH.

THE BRIDE'S HOUSE.

THE KING, THE BRIDE, THE CHORUS OF VIRGINS,
THE BRIDE'S BROTHERS.

THE CHORUS.

Who cometh up from the wilderness,
Leaning on her Beloved?

THE KING.

Underneath this apple-tree I found thee,
Within its shade first wakened thee to love,
Here received thee from her hand who bare thee.

THE BRIDE.

Set me as a seal upon thy heart—
Set me as a seal upon thy arm—
For cruel as the grave is jealousy,
　　But strong as death is love!
　　Its flames are flames of fire
　　Whose most vehement heat
　　Great waters cannot quench.
　　Nor can the floods o'erwhelm.
　　Though one should give his all
　　In hope to buy such love,
　　With scorn would he be scorned!

Set me as a seal upon thy heart—
Set me as a seal upon thy arm—
For cruel as the grave is jealousy,
　　And strong as death is love!

THE BRIDE'S BROTHERS.

　　We have a little sister,
　　All immature her charms—
　　What answer shall we give
　　When the bridegroom calleth?
　　Then, if she be a wall,

We will build upon her
A palace of pure silver ;
But if she be a door,
Then will we enclose her
In a house of cedar.

THE BRIDE.

Behold ! I am a wall,
A tower my chastity !
Thus did I favor find
In the eyes that sought me,
And thus did I find peace,
And my Beloved, peace.

Solomon had a vineyard,
And let it out to keepers ;
Every one was to bring him
For his share of the vintage
A thousand marks of silver.

My vineyard, which is mine,
Have I still before me :
Thou, Solomon, must have
As thine the thousand pieces ;

The keepers of the fruit
Shall have but two hundred.

The King.

Thou that dwellest in the gardens ;
Thy companions hear thy voice,—
Cause me to hear it.

The Bride *sings.*

Make haste, my Beloved !
And be like a roe,
Or like a young hart
On the mountains of spice.

Exeunt omnes.

A Visit to Santa Claus.

THIS little poem was written for the amusement of my own children, and I offer it to the thousands of children to whom Christmas is a joyous season. All those for whom it was written are in Paradise.

Come sit by the fireside, dearest,
　With wee Helen on your knee,
While Maude draws up the footstool,
　And Hope abides with me ;
A boy of the rarest promise,
　A girl full of childish glee,
And prattling bright-eyed Helen,
　Making the magic three ;
Three in the social circle,
　And Kate in the home above ;
But here let us all be joyous,
　And there let us all be love.
'Tis now on the eve of Christmas,

When the Saviour came on earth,
'Twill soon be the gladsome hour
  That told of the glorious birth ;
When the Star in the East was rising,
  And the Angel bands came forth,
Proclaiming with sweet voices,
  Good-will and peace on earth.
When the air was filled with music,
  And the night was aglow with light,
Which the shepherds saw with gladness,
  But the kings with sore affright.

They knew not then that Jesus,
  The glorious King of Kings,
Sought not an earthly sceptre
  Which station with it brings ;
Nor knew they that His kingdom
  Was not a spot of earth,
But o'er the undying spirit,
  Cleansed by a second birth,
He sought to rule if haply,
  The world the call would hear,
And to His heavenly teaching
  Turn yet a listening ear.

But now the world rejoices,
  The shepherds *and* the kings,
That God a pardon offers
  And Christ the pardon brings!

So that is the reason, Papa,
  Said little wondering Maude,
We should all be glad at Christmas
  And send good things abroad.
And that is the reason, Papa,
  Said Hope with bright'ning eye,
That Santa Claus is coming
  With good things by and by;
And now you said you'd tell us
  How you went the other night,
To Santa Claus's workshop
  To see if my sled was right;
And to speak for a doll for Maude
  That could open and shut its eyes,
And about the many pretty things
  He made for the girls and boys.

I'll tell you the story briefly,
  And then you must off to bed,

For Santa Claus will be coming
  With a load upon your sled ;
And if you still are watching
  I fear he may go by,
For he's a curious fellow,
  And does things on the sly.

So all began to listen,
  And the kitten oped her eyes
And gazed round the circle
  With an innocent surprise.
Across her drowsy eyelids
  The nimble cricket ran,
And in the general silence
  The story thus began.

On a dark and cloudy night,
  With a howling northeast storm,
Not a star to give me light,
  Nor a cloak to keep me warm,
Not a path to guide my feet
  To his high and safe retreat,
Up the dark and lonesome ravine,
  Step by step I picked my way,

By a little murmuring runlet
   I had often tracked by day,
And which led to Santa Claus',
   I had heard my Grandpa say.
For this was the only evening
   In the whole revolving year
His deep hidden mountain home
   To a mortal would appear.
'Twas the night of Hallowe'en,
Night on which strange things are seen.
And it was on Friday, too,
   Saddest day of all the seven,
And the moon was in the wane,
   And the hour beyond eleven !
Fearful night ! On every hillside
   Troops of fairies dance and sing,
And with sound of merry music
   Charm the mortal to the ring ;
Witches ride upon the broomstick,
   Wizards conjure visions dire,
Warlocks revel in the tempest
   Every moment growing higher ;
Bird and beast are ill at ease,
   Screams are heard in upper air

Voices whisper in the trees,
  Life and sound are everywhere ;—
But the darkness and the bluster
  Hide the shapes from human eye,
Though you feel them every moment
  As they swiftly hurry by.

You must choose, he always said,
Such a night, so drear and dread ;
If it should be calm and still,
All is darkness on the hill,
And no mortal man can find
Cave of Santa Claus the kind.
But when fierce and swift the wind
Drives the dark storm-cloud along,
And still blacker grows the night
And more loud the tempest's song,
Then a twinkling light they say,
Guides the traveller on his way.

So I started for the mountains,
Where, he said, Old Santa Claus,
Deep within a rocky cavern,
  All secure from colds and thaws,

Daily, with unceasing labor,
 Wrought the constant livelong year,
Just to give the prattling youngsters
 Their merry Christmas cheer.
I stumbled o'er the bowlders,
 I slipped upon the ice ;
The owls all fell to hooting,
 And I thought that in a trice
They would perch upon my shoulders,
 Flap their wings about my ears,
Call their old familiar goblin
 From the hollow haunted tree,
And drive me from the mountain,
 So I should not get to see
Old Santa Claus' workshop,
 And his team of eight reindeers.

I stood and peered around me,
 And far up the rocky glen
I saw a glimmering taper,
 So I travelled on again.
An hour or more I battled,
 And the storm still louder blew,
Until full faint and weary

With the lengthened way I grew;
The light still danced before me,
    But the owls kept up their cry,
And the pine-trees' swaying branches,
    Moaning as the wind swept by,
Made the path more wild and eerie
And the night more dread and dreary,
And the tempest loud and high
Hurled the clouds along the sky,
And the topmost branches broke
From the brittle chestnut oak.
But I struggled on amain
Through the cold and pelting rain;
And the light which like a star
Twinkled, twinkled from afar,
As I nearer to it came
Seemed to burn with steadier flame.
I crept forward quietly,
    Over log and rut and stone,
Thought I saw the rocky doorway
    Whence the little taper shone,
When an owl with great ado,
Flapped his wings and cried, " t'whoo !"

The light went out—alone I stood,
Wet and weary in the wood ;
And I called with all my might,
" Santa Claus ! please make a light ! "
Still the owl around me flew,
Screaming out, " t'whit ! t'whoo ! "
Ere I had a minute stood,
Santa Claus, the kind and good,
    Wondering at the rout and din,
Came with torch of good pine wood
    And politely asked me in ;
And the Owl, with staring eyes,
Seeming as in great surprise,
To his hollow tree once more,
Close beside the cavern door,
Staring at me still, withdrew,
Settled down, and said " t'whoo ! "

So beside a rousing fire
    Santa Claus and I sat down,
And I warmed my toes and fingers
    And he asked about the town ;
Wondered who had little babies
    Old enough to play with toys,

Said he knew about the other,
  Bigger little girls and boys.
He had piles of sleds and things
Hanging in his little shop,
Which he said he meant to trade
For some things he never made,
So there would be variety
On the welcome Christmas-tree.

Then he pointed out the sleigh
That he rode in, on his way
Round the world on Christmas-eve,
Lined with furs and snug and tight ;
Then the stable came in view
Where the little reindeers were,
And they stamped and snorted too
When they saw a stranger near,
And their little eyes looked bright
In the blazing pine torch-light.

Santa Claus just shook his finger
  And they stood as still as mice,
And we passed along behind them
  To a little room so nice ;

And there, very busy knitting,
Mrs. Santa Claus was sitting ;
And around were dolls and mittens
Waxen dogs and sugar kittens,
Lots of ribbons, braids, and laces,
Albums, music-boxes, vases—
Everything, and ten times more
Than you'd think of in an hour.

So she handed me a chair
　　Close beside the chimney fire,
And of all the men and maidens
　　In the town she did inquire ;
Asked me who were getting married,
　　What the winter fashions were ;
Calling for a full description
　　Of the modern female wear—
Flounces, nets, hoop-skirts and laces,
　　She could understand them all ;
But I had a dreadful trouble
　　To explain the " water-fall ; "
And when to another feature
　　The description did extend,
And I tried to give a notion

Of a full-grown " Grecian bend,"
Just to see the dear good lady,
  With her fine, expressive face,
Smiling half, and half resenting
  Fashions going such a pace—
And old Santa Claus, the jovial,
  With his pipe between his teeth,
While around his head was curling
  From its bowl a beauteous wreath ;
One eye shut and t'other winking
  Kindly at me through the smoke,
As if he was surely thinking
  What a most tremendous joke
I was telling the old lady—
  Was a picture I can tell you,
Such as you may never see :
But I urged that it was true,
And no joke at all of mine ;
But he only winked the more,
Rolling o'er the parlor floor,
Laughing till his sides were sore.

Much to talk he did incline,
So he ordered up some wine,

Cakes, and nuts, and apples too ;
And as well-bred people do,
Drink, said he, and eat your fill,
For the night is damp and chill,
And there's many a weary mile
    Of rock and ravine to be strode
Ere you reach the little stile
    Leading to the Bloomsburg road.
Well, we had a merry chat,
Talked of this and then of that ;
But at last the clock struck two,
And I knew it would not do
To be seen in morning chill
On old Santa Claus' hill :
So I buttoned up my coat
Close around my breast and throat,
Drew my cap about my ears,
Turned to bid them both "good-night"—
    .   .   Out went the light—
            And there I stood
In the dark and lonesome wood.
Not an object could I see
    But the owl with staring eyes
Peering from his hollow tree,

Santa Claus' watchman he ;
And again he flaps his wings,
And again he loudly cries
" T'whit ! t'whit ! t'whoo-oo-oo !"
  For a moment I stood still,
Scarcely knowing what to do ;
  When I started down the hill—
  And along the rocky glen,
  As I travelled home again,
  Sending through me many a chill,
Came the owl's " t'whit ! t'whoo-oo-oo !"

Saint Valentine's Day.

IN times whereof man's memory
  Doth not contrary run,
The festive sporting of this day
  Already had begun.
On England's shores, on Scotland's hills,
  In France's sunny vales,
The custom has long since prevailed—
  Aye, and it now prevails.
Now many an eye is sonneted,
  And many a ringlet sung,
And tokens of respect and love
  Are sent from old and young;
For man learned of the birds that choose
  A mate upon this day,
And now trim up their ruffled plumes
  And once again look gay.
Although for months unused to sing,
  Kind nature breaks the spell,
The love and hope so long pent up—

How aptly they will tell;
With arching neck, and roguish eye,
And plumage spruce and fine,
With soft and gently cooing voice
They sing a Valentine.

What pretty coquetry is there,
And with what female art
The coy young birdlings seek the grove
And guard the yielding heart;
And though they hear, will not attend
Their lover's glowing strain,
But, busied with a ruffled plume,
Affect a slight disdain;
And careless thus to wound a heart
With coquetry, they dare
To ask another young gallant
The boon of love to share.
With glossy neck, and leering eye,
And feathers flaunting gay,
They hop about from branch to branch
And make a grand display;
With graceful motion, easy mien,
Yet coy and bashful glance,

In the deep woods they hide their charms
  As if by merest chance :
The bough that half conceals the form
  Lays open the design,
Which is, in truth, to coax a youth
  To sing a Valentine.

But whether birds all know this fact
  I can't pretend to say ;
I wish they did—'twould give them great
  Success throughout the day ;
And since we see the female kind
  Undoubted art employ,
'Tis only fair to predicate
  That all know how to toy.
Now all the arts Dame Nature taught
  By each is brought to bear—
A symmetry of face and form
  Is prayed for by the fair ;
And though they may coquette at noon,
  By eve that mood is past,
For those who take not mates to-day
  Must die old maids at last.
So though despair awhile may cast

The gallant suitors down,
Yet in the end love with success
  Will all their trials crown.
And thus we see upon this day
  'Tis Nature's grand design
That those who love should tell their love
  And choose a Valentine.

From Nature thus mankind have learned
  The uses of the day,
And many a missive charged with love
  Is speeding on its way,
And many a nameless billet-doux,
  By fairy fingers penned,
Makes the blood tingle in the veins
  Of lover or of friend.
The timid wooer tells his tale,
  The bashful maid can write—
Feelings long pent within the breast
  This day brings forth to light ;
For each one has the privilege
  The plaintive verse to twine,
And from the fairest, noblest ones
  To choose a Valentine.

The love a maiden dare not speak
  Can thus be all confessed,
And sentiments but now made known
  May warm a mutual breast;
And Cupid has throughout the land
  Devices quaint and rare
By which this secret of the heart
  Is told by ladies fair.
Two billing doves, two piercèd hearts
  The tale of love can tell,
A little line, a simple word
  Can make the bosom swell;
A rosebud will a flame declare,
  But do not lightly twine
A sprig of myrtle in a wreath
  That asks a Valentine.

'Tis thus the frolic birds of air
  Upon this sacred day
Choose a companion who shall drive
  The cares of life away,
With whom to spend the summer months
  Till winter comes again,
But part to meet no more on earth

Ere bleak December's rain.
But not so will I choose my love—
  We never more will part :
In heat or cold I'll wear her
  Ever nearest to my heart ;
For if she will but bless my suit
  I'll never more repine,
And from that day forever forth
  Will be her Valentine.

THE VALENTINE.

Not only in the spring of life,
  When young and gay,
Thy ruby lips with kisses rife
  Are Cupid's stay ;
Not only when the blushing rose
  Strives in thy cheek,
Not only when thy bright eye glows
  Thy love I seek.

But when December's snow and rain
  O'ercloud the sky,

To thee, as in the spring, again
  I'd gladly fly ;
Not like the birds, when summer's o'er
  Would I resign
One who long cheered the sultry hour—
  My Valentine.

The Breach of Promise.

 AN CUPID, passing by one day
In musing mood more grave than
gay,
I, feeling greatly wronged and
grieved,
And by a neighbor much deceived,
Begged him to be concerned for me
And issue forth a præcipe,
And bring to court without delay,
By capias, one Maggie May;
And then proceeded to impart,
With eyes suffused and beating heart,
The various hurts and wrongs that she,
For many years, had done to me.
He took my statement and passed on,
Saying that justice should be done;
That he would put in legal phrase
My whole complaint ere many days,
And nothing intermit or stay

To bring to justice Maggie May.
  Nor did he in the least defer.
Before a month had passed around,
Forth came his scented messenger
With modest packet, silken bound,
And, hid within its legal fold
The writ of capias lay enrolled,
Embossed with quaint devices rare,
Formed to conciliate the fair
And pleasant to the eyes to see :
Two doves, two hearts, a canopy,
A silver dart, a diamond ring,
A house on fashion's avenue
With church and opera in view,
And many another beauteous thing
Which wily Cupid knew full well
Would make the female bosom swell.
And making scarce a moment stay
To serve the writ, passed on his way,
But left with me the formal charge
That Cupid had drawn out at large,
And to be filed without delay,
Whereby full justice should have play
Against the wiles of Maggie May ;

And thus did my attorney say :—
  "Columbia County, double S.,
In County Court of Common Pleas,
Number fifteen of Term of June,
In eighteen hundred seventy-one.
  Miss Maggie May, a spinster gay,
Was held to answer, *sans* delay,
One Simon Lovesick of a plea
Of trespass on the case upon
Her promises, and wherefore she
Hath borne herself so haughtily
Toward the plaintiff : whereupon
In the said court, in doleful strains,
By Cupid, his attorney, he,
Said Simon, of her thus complains.
  For that whereas said Maggie May
Long heretofore, that is to say
On February the fourteenth day,
In eighteen hundred sixty-nine,
Much to said Simon did incline,
Chose him to be her valentine,
And more to bind him then and there
Gave to him, of her golden hair,
A well-wrought bracelet for his wear,

And in the view of other girls
Allowing his toying with her curls,
And when the party broke to go,
To tie her ribbons in a bow,
And as they through the moonlight went
Upon his arm full kindly leant,
And left her taper fingers stay
Within his grasp the livelong way ;
And though he often to his lips
Pressed lovingly her finger-tips,
No rising frown could one espy,
But downcast was her brilliant eye
And flushed her cheek with crimson dye ;
And in a certain sweet discourse
Held then and there betwixt them two,
When Simon asked her him to wed,
The self-same Maggie aforesaid
Promised, without or guile or force,
When she should be required thereto,
To go with Simon to the church,
And there before the holy man,
And eke a goodlie companie,
To give and place her lily hand
Within the sacred marriage band,

And wear for aye the wedding-ring
Which Simon with him was to bring.
But when required to name the day
The false and fickle Maggie May,
Leaving said Simon in the lurch,
Would always say her lover nay,
While he hath ever had and still
Firmly retains the self-same will
His first said promise to fulfil.

And afterward, that is to say,
Upon the same aforesaid day,
With the said Simon, her said beau,
Beneath the sacred mistletoe
Said Maggie willingly did go
And pledge him with a nectared kiss,
To be thenceforth forever his,
And him unto his dying day
To love, and honor, and obey ;
To him to give her hand and heart
And never, never from him part ;
But with her bridemaids to repair
To parish church and meet him there,
Upon that morning when the fair

Early their sleepy couch eschew
To bathe them in the May-day dew:
And Simon there without delay
Promised to meet said Maggie May,
On the aforesaid first of May,
At parish church at dawn of day,
And her to wed for aye and aye.

And his aforesaid promise he,
Said Simon, kept religiously ;
And at the church at stated hour
Arrived with chariot and four,
And many friends had with him sped
To see the lovesick Simon wed,
And at the church-door tarried long
For the said Maggie and her throng.
The surpliced priest was waiting there
Clasping the Book of Common Prayer,
And all the friends, maliciously,
From sun to sun, that blessed day,
With jeers and laughter stayed to see
Said Simon wed said Maggie May.

Nevertheless, said Maggie May
Upon the last aforesaid day,

Did her said promise not regard,
But falsified her plighted word
And troth, in form aforesaid made,
And all her promises gainsaid ;
Designing, with a wicked heart,
Upon said Simon to impose,
And never to perform the part
She with him had agreed in those
Delicious moments when they stood,
With meeting lips and bounding blood,
Beneath the sacred mistletoe
On that said evening long ago ;
But craftily and subtly
Him to deceive intending, she
Yet the said Simon hath not wed,
As she was clearly bound to do
By her said promise aforesaid.

And although often afterward,
That is to say the day and year
Aforesaid, out of pure regard
The aforesaid Simon did appear
And humbly beg said Maggie May
To name for them the nuptial day,

She him to take as wedded spouse
Still hath refused and doth refuse.
Whereby a damage doth redound
To Simon of ten thousand pound,
And while his heart with anguish wrings,
To ease the smart his suit he brings."

𝔇estiny.

A Portuguese Tradition.

THERE is a tradition among the Portuguese that certain precious stones rule particular months, and confer upon persons born under their influence certain qualities of body and of mind. According to the authority before us, they are connected in the following manner :

JANUARY. .... *Jasper*....... ...... Constancy and fidelity.

FEBRUARY .... *Amethyst*............ This stone preserves from strong passions, and insures peace of mind.

MARCH....... *Bloodstone* .... Insures courage and success in hazardous enterprises.

APRIL........ *Sapphire Diamond* .... Repentance and innocence.

MAY .... *Emerald* .... Success in love.

JUNE........ *Legate* .... Long life and health.

JULY........ *Cornelian Ruby* .... The forgetfulness of evils arising from broken friendship or faithless love.

AUGUST...... *Sardonyx* .... Conjugal fidelity.

SEPTEMBER.. *Chrysolite* .... Preserves from or cures folly.

OCTOBER..... *Opal* .... Misfortune and hope.

NOVEMBER... *Topaz* .... Fidelity in friendship.

DECEMBER... *Turquoise*............. The most brilliant success in every enterprise or circumstance in life. " He who possesses a Turquoise is always sure of his friends."

IT has been said that life's a dream,
    That things are not just what they
        seem,
        And that, in truth, we only think
We dress ourselves or take a drink ;
That we are all somnambulists,
That everything by chance exists,
And not a mortal e'er can know
Whence he hath come or where he'll go ;
That we may well say, " Mother Earth,"
Of her from whom we had our birth,
From whom, by daily toil and strife,
We draw the substance of our life,
Upon whose bosom, when we die,
In deep unbroken sleep we'll lie ;
Whilst she, a living, breathing thing,
Rolling forever in her ring,
Sees us, poor animalculæ,
Mere little creatures of a day,
Come, storm an hour, then go away !

To Sheol—Doth the Hebrew say,
And mean the grave ? or that drear place,
Where the departed, for a space

Await in trembling and in fear,
What time the judgment shall appear?

To Hades—Asks the polished Greek,
And fields elysian, there to seek
Sages and heroes and the great
Who passed their life in kingly state?—
Or else, to fire and chains accurst,
Or punished with eternal thirst,
Or, as the endless ages run,
Have constant labor still undone?

Or, with the scoffing Sadducee,
Deny that man shall ever be
From Sheol called, from Hades brought,
To give account of deed or thought?

Or, as the latest teachers hold,
That man, though formed of earthly mould,
In holy hope and grace divine
Shall hence in radiant beauty shine,
And tread the Psalmist's glorious way
In progress toward the Perfect Day!
But if, contemned this grace divine,

To "Mother Earth" he shall incline,
And buried in her quiet breast,
Seek there an everlasting rest;
When comes the last undying fire,
Expiring, he shall not expire!

But be that as it may, we see
Man has a ruling destiny;
In proof of which, the spangled sky
Spreads to our eyes her lights on high,
And when bright science raised the veil
Astrology could tell a tale,
And drawing knowledge from afar,
Reveal a fate in every star.
But, 't is not by the stars alone
The destiny of man is known,
For the dark mine holds many a gem,
Potent the ills of life to stem;
And every month has some one stone
By fate selected as its own—
A talisman the good to guard,
A charm the ills of life to ward.

I.

She who is born when the young year,
　　Just starting, springs from chaos' arms,
Receives a *Jasper* bright and clear,
　　Patron of virtue's highest charms.
Implicitly rely on her;
　　A bright example shall she be,
For this upon her shall confer
　　Fidelity and constancy.

II.

The second month is joined by fate
　　With *Amethyst* of violet hue,
And if thou here wouldst seek a mate,
　　I warrant her a partner true.
To these no fickle airs belong,
　　They are not foolish, harsh, unkind;
This stone secures from passions strong,
　　And grants them peace of mind.

III.

Wouldst thou seek one courageous, firm,
　　One to protect when dangers lower,

One in decision prompt and stern,
  Yet kind with all his power?
The third month and the bright *Bloodstone*
  Insure both courage and success.
Seek him : when to his arms thou'st flown,
  Thou ne'er wilt love him less.

IV.

The *Sapphire Diamond* reigns supreme
  O'er the fourth month of every year,
And he will still preserve esteem
  Who dates his birthday here.
He will repent all evils done,
  And kindness will dispense,
And truly at your feet lay down
  A heart of innocence.

V.

Know'st thou a mind pure, firm, and true,
  A mind of strength and worth ?
Wouldst thou possess this jewel too,
  Found seldom on this earth ?
Go, seek with hope—the *Emerald's* thine—

Go, all thy doubts remove ;
It is the earnest and the sign
Of full success in love.

VI.

Say, dost thou wish for life and health,
    The pleasures which on them await?
The comforts and the joys of wealth
    Which still attend the great,
That when old age has bared thy head,
    Thy limbs should yet feel youth ?
Rejoice that thus thy lot has sped—
    The *Legate* gives them both.

VII.

If thou hast loved with all thy soul,
    As young and artless beings love,
And been deceived, shake off control—
    The *Ruby* all thy care removes.
How deep so-e'er the sting has gone
    Thy talisman can heal the smart,
For with it comes, when all have flown,
    Forgetfulness of heart.

VIII.

A faithful and a loving mate
　　Is better than the brightest gem
That in the pride of sovereign state
　　Glitters in regal diadem.
Wouldst thou have such to share thy heart?
　　Then in this month thy search should be ;
Here doth the *Sardonyx* impart
　　True conjugal fidelity.

IX.

If thou by any froward deed
　　Hast caused a tender heart to break,
By inadvertence made to bleed
　　A tender bosom for thy sake,
Take courage yet—bear up in spite
　　Of the dark brow of melancholy ;
The triumph's thine—the *Chrysolite*
　　Completely cures from folly.

X.

Has stern misfortune weighed thee down,
　　And pressed thee with a heavy hand ?

Bear up beneath her boding frown ;
  Let faith and love thy hope expand.
The *Opal* guides thy course in life,
  Gives power with all its storms to cope,
And says, in tumult and in strife,
  And in misfortune, hope.

XI.

Wouldst have a friend more kind and true
  In cheerless poverty than power,
Whose bands of friendship closer drew
  As more the tempests lower ?
Seek him upon whose natal hour
  Her yellow light the *Topaz* threw,
For in that heart thou'lt find a dower
  Richer than all Peru.

XII.

But thou art he o'er whose charmed life
  The gems have thrown the brightest fate,
The truest friends, the kindest wife,
  Success in enterprises great.

Thine is the *Turquoise*—go, thy friends
Will ne'er desert—thy life shall be
Bright as the sun when he ascends,
Calm as his setting on the sea.

Vanity of Greatness.

 EACE, commerce, arts! long may your
  cares beguile,
  And ripening crops along the valleys
  smile,
And Nature answering culture kindly give
With an unsparing hand the means to live ;
Beneath your sway no shrilly sounding horn
Wakes with its early noise the breezy morn ;
No rumbling drum, nor cannon fraught with
  death,
Strikes the quick ear or takes the laboring breath ;
But the shrill cock proclaims the infant day
When in the East the clouds look scarcely gray.
No longer does the sun from mountain height
Shed his first beams on bayonets sparkling bright,
But kindly pours upon the smiling land
Fruits, flowers, and blessings with a liberal hand.
 Say, is he happier, did we know the heart,
Who leans on others for his sole support,

Than the bold man who independent stands
And by his labor tills his generous lands ?
Who knows no wants but those which nature
　　knows,
Who flatters not his friends nor fears his foes ?
No : Nature will reverse no one decree—
He is a freeman whom the truth makes free ;
And he is happiest who supports himself,
Both unambitious of renown or pelf,
Nor asks for homage in the motley crowd
Where heads most empty always are most loud.
　Can sounding titles, a mere empty name
Blunt the sharp shaft the sons of envy aim,
Smooth the rough pillow, racking pains assuage,
Or keep aloof the iron hand of age ?
Will never pain or sickness cloud the brow
That glitters with the diamond brightly now ?
Beneath that smile is there no secret woe,
Or does rank chase all ills from all below ?
No : let his titles sound however high,
The wingéd taunt and slander round them fly ;
Eternal torment and unreasoning hate
Are both companions of unwieldy state,
And whether merit or a bribe has raised,

He still by some is flouted, some is praised.
Nor is he happier who, to greatness born,
Fails in his place and reaps the world's wild scorn ;
Far better he who, having nobly dared,
Proves the divinity the race has shared.
  The world's great chieftain, when the world
    was gained,
Wept as he thought no other one remained ;
Wept as he saw his labor at an end,
And nothing left to conquer or defend.
The soaring warrior, fell at once to earth,
Proved to the world the baseness of his birth ;
He seized the bowl, and in debauch expired
That conquering spirit which the world had fired,
He seized the bowl and gave his mighty mind
To pleasure and to riot unconfined :
He who in life had sternly sought and won
A wider empire than his Macedon,
What joys to him did all his victories bring—
What better is the world that he was king ?
He left a large, corrupt, unwieldy state,
Cool friends, warm enemies, the title *great !*
  When England's Queen, the haughty and the
    proud,

By age, by sickness, and by grief was bowed,
Though long she swayed, with an imperious
    hand
And lofty brow, the sceptre of command ;
Though she had made a name without decay,
Revered for deeds that cannot fade away—
When Death, the monarch, brooked no more
    delay,
She would have given an empire for a day.
"Oh," she exclaimed, as died the clock's sad
    chime,
"I would give millions for an inch of time !"
Count ye that fabulous which gossips tell,
That she had loved, not wisely, but too well—
That Essex's fate weighed her worn spirit down,
And she must feel a love she dared not own,
And while a foe kept back the fatal ring
Of unrequited love she felt the sting ;
Vowed fell revenge, and played a sovereign's
    part,
Sad, sighing, signed, but signed with broken
    heart ;
That when he fell, and honor's flag was furled,
The last cord snapt that bound her to the world ;

Crying in anguish o'er the well-laid plot,
" May God forgive you, Countess, I cannot ? "

Behold the bold adventurer of France,
Whose nod the world but waited to advance ;
Whose sharp eye glanced along the dusty plain
And counted thousands by his orders slain ;
He at whose name old men forgot their years
And shouted, "Vive l'Empereur !" with joyous
    tears ;
Held by the French the high, the mighty mind,
The great grand climax of all human kind ;
To whom to plan and conquer were the same,
Whose spirit high disaster could not tame ;
He fiercely tost upon the shoals is cast,
Far from his chosen home he breathes his last ;
With scarce a friendly hand to close his eyes,
The first, great Emperor Napoleon dies !
He raves of empire with his latest breath,
And proves the ruling passion strong in death.
He dies, a life of care and toil is sped,
And he is numbered with the glorious dead ;
Above his dust let monuments arise,
And with their glittering spires assault the skies ;

Let a whole nation weep upon his hearse,
And poets consecrate the epic verse ;
Still shall the tear bedew the widow's cheek
And mourn a name she hardly dares to speak ;
Still must the orphan for a father sigh,
And while smiles light his cheek tears dim his
    eye.
And thus, though praised, caressed, beloved by
    all,
From his great height he did a captive fall ;
Unhappy he when in his towering pride,
Consumed by wishes yet unsatisfied,
And still unhappy, listening to the roar
Of the great ocean on Helena's shore.

  And England's Charles could tell if there can
    be
A life of greatness without misery.
Born to a throne, he came in pomp and power
To play upon the stage his fitful hour ;
Unequal to his part he forth was led,
Cursed, wept, and honored, to a gory bed ;
And Cromwell rose and ruled the hapless land
With verse and cant, and cimetar and brand,

Yet ruled it ably.   With a statesman's hand
He sways the sceptre of supreme command,
Fulfilling of his dream the high behest,
"Although not King of England, still the best."
Was the *Protector* happier in his lot
Than plain and sturdy Cromwell?   I trow not.
For when above an awe-struck land he swayed,
Red with his sovereign's blood, his conquering
    blade,
He feared the assassin's knife, the poisoner's
    bowl,
Nor trusted those whom but their fears control.
Not all the good he did the commonweal—
And none have shown for it more honest zeal—
Nor gloomy death, nor Milton's glowing pen,
Could save his bones from hands of ruthless men
When the great spirit soared from mortal ken.

    Thus all seek happiness.   How few there be
Who the right way among these windings see.
It cannot be with him whose restless mind
Is striving still to overtop mankind,
Nor does he find it who has once attained
The envied height and there till death remained ;

E'en he has sighed for freedom and repose,
And the low station whence at first he rose.
  Though not to greatness is true bliss con-
    signed,
It is not given to that barbarous hind
Who knows no want beyond the present hour,
And no superiority but power ;
Whose low delights are sensual, not refined,
Who has no joys in common with the mind ;
For pleasure is not happiness.   We know
The one is common to all things below,
The other to mankind alone is given,
A pledge of immortality and heaven.
  Nor is it found where want with mournful face
Holds at the board his ever-present place.
Poets may prate of love in cottage bred,
A glass of water and a crust of bread,
And paint, with all the fancy of the race,
A walk by moonlight, and a pretty face,
A flowery garden, sombre forest trees,
The song of birds, the gentle evening breeze,
And all the wondrous panoply of charms
Their fine imagination breeds and warms ;
Yet poverty, disguise it as they may,

Brings far more griefs than joys in its array.
  Then wouldst thou know where happiness is
    found—
In what bright region, on what hallowed ground,
If not among the revels of the great,
Enthroned in majesty and pomp and state,
Nor where grim poverty, with pinching face,
At sufferance lives, the pensioner of grace?
Then mark me well — this bliss 'tis yours to
    know—
Who would be happy must make others so!
And e'en a smile, a sigh, a kindly word,
Full oft has gladness to the breast restored.
It costs not to be kind—let kindness reign;
It doubles pleasure, lessens every pain.
Relieve distress, and let your hand run o'er
In generous kindness to the needy poor;
Thus when the joy of others you secure,
Your happiness is thereby doubly sure.
  Content be with your lot, for God will care
And kindly answer every heartfelt prayer;
He hears the raven's cry, and shall not He
Supply your wants and your distresses see?
Still let your home of all the world be found

The spot where smiles and wit and love abound.
There let your kindness and your tone reveal
That though a husband, you're a lover still;
For there alone true happiness shall dwell
Where kindred spirits wisely love, and well.
Scorn of parade and pomp the unmeaning noise,
And seek in quiet home for purer joys,
And there secure a pleasure unalloyed
With selfish thoughts, unsated and uncloyed.

Rape of Dearbhorgil.

THE ballad is founded upon an event of most melancholy importance to Ireland, if, as we are told by the Irish historians, it gave England the first opportunity of profiting by their dissensions and of subduing them. Ireland was at this time (about 1160) divided into a number of petty principalities—five at least—each of which was governed by its own prince, sometimes hereditary, though more frequently gaining position by usurpation and the power of the sword ; and over the whole reigned a monarch, generally elected by the chiefs of the different principalities.

It may be easily imagined that the crown did not rest very firmly on the head of anyone, and that rapine, murder, and bloodshed were the order of the day. With no power to restrain and no law to punish, might became right and the sword was king.

Such was the state of affairs in Ireland when the events occurred which form the groundwork of the ballad. O'Halloran relates the circumstances as follows : '' The King of Leinster had long conceived a violent affection for Dearbhorgil, daughter of the King of Meath, and though she had been for some time married to O'Ruark, Prince of Breffni, yet it could not restrain his passion. They carried on a private correspondence, and she informed him that O'Ruark intended soon to go on a pilgrimage (an act of piety frequent in those days), and conjured him to embrace that opportunity of conveying her from a husband she detested to a lover she adored. MacMurchad too punctually obeyed the summons, and had the lady conveyed to his capital of Ferns.

'' The monarch, Roderick, espoused the cause of O'Ruark, and they drove MacMurchad from his dominions. He fled to England and obtained from Henry II. letters permitting any of his subjects to engage with MacMurchad in the enterprise against

Ireland. A considerable force was soon mustered, and both parties prepared to take the field. Dissensions and bribes soon weakened the Irish ; and Roderick, finding himself unable to maintain the combat, surrendered. It was a long time after, however, before the conquest was considered complete, but the English had gained a foothold, and there was not patriotism enough left to expel the 'ruthless invader.'

"While MacMurchad was in England Dearbhorgil entered the Convent of St. Bridget, at Kildare. MacMurchad died in the year 1771, four years after he had carried off the Princess of Breffni. O'Ruark was assassinated at a conference between him and Hugh de Lacy, by his own nephew, Gryffyth, in 1172."

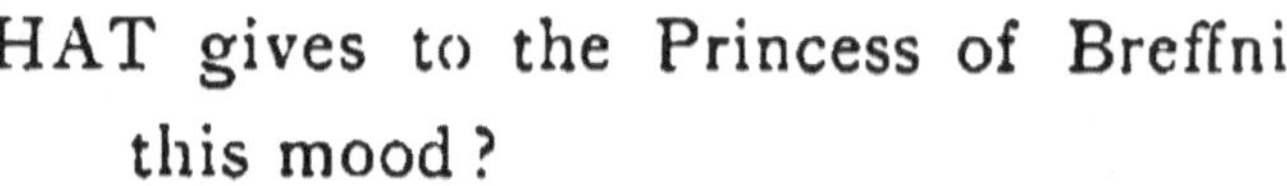

WHAT gives to the Princess of Breffni
　　this mood ?
Why seeks she so often unblest soli-
　　tude ?
From morning till night on the turret she walks,
She gazes on vacancy, vacantly talks,
Or sings with low voice, as the day wears along,
To calm her wrought spirit, some snatches of
　　song;
O'Ruark has far on a pilgrimage gone,
And his lady now sighs in the castle alone.

No one to console her, she pensively sees
Birds courting their mates on the blossoming
　　trees ;

All nature looks gay in the flowering spring—
The insects, bedizened with gold, are on wing;
The butterfly tribe sport from flower to flower,
In pleasure and love pass the sunshiny hour;
But O'Ruark has far on a pilgrimage gone,
And his lady now sighs in the castle alone.

'Tis sad thus to count every hour of the day,
And then think of weeks when one's love is
　　away;
When the sun in the evening sinks down in the
　　West,
How sweet in the arms of a dear one to rest:
No wonder the lady so pensively roved,
For absent was he whom she tenderly loved;
O'Ruark had far on a pilgrimage gone,
And Dearbhorgil now sighed in the castle alone.

Oh does she so speedily wish his return?
For him does her eye now so languidly burn?
Is it grief that has faded the rose on her cheek?
Do watching and weeping their wild work here
　　speak?
'Tis watching, 'tis weeping, anxiety, care,

That give to the lady so restless an air ;
For O'Ruark has far on a pilgrimage gone,
And Dearbhorgil now sighs in the castle alone.

What flushes her cheek as she looks o'er the
    plain ?
What brightens her eye ? 'tis that cavalier train
That gaily caparisoned rides through the wood,
Which changes so quickly the fair lady's mood.
The foremost rides fleetly, his steed is well tried,
A chaperoned palfrey is led by its side :
O'Ruark has far on a pilgrimage gone,
And Dearbhorgil now sighs in the castle alone.

She waves him her kerchief, the signal he
    knows,
And straight to the hall of the castle goes,
Unbinds the gay palfrey and carelessly throws
The rein on its neck, all regardless of foes ;
Dismounting he raps with the hilt of his sword
And calls to the warder, "Ho ! where is thy
    lord ?"
"O'Ruark has far on a pilgrimage gone,
And my lady now sighs in the castle alone."

"Then call me thy lady," thus spoke the bold
    chief,
MacMurchad of Leinster.   "Be prompt and be
    brief.
My retainers are yonder, and here is my sword."
Throughout the whole castle like fire flew the
    word,
" MacMurchad is waiting below at the hall—
Send thither the guardsmen and arm one and all ;
For our lord has afar on a pilgrimage gone,
And our lady shall sigh in the castle alone."

The lady came not : he impatiently blew
A note on his bugle ; a squire to him flew ;
He flung him the reins, then strode to the hall ;
The lady was ready and waiting his call ;
The guard circle round her, he reaches the door,
And two of the foremost lie stiff in their gore ;
All their efforts are vain, for Dearbhorgil is gone,
And O'Ruark may sigh in his castle alone.

O lightly, I ween, to the saddle she sprung,
On the neck of her courser the reins loosely
    hung ;

They waved an adieu as they rode from the door;
O'Ruark shall see his young bride nevermore,
For swiftly in flight over hillside and plain
Their steeds bravely bear them; pursuit is in
    vain;
Their retainers are near them, for valor enrolled :
"Those who join us shall stay," says MacMur-
    chad the bold.
And though there was arming for fight to prepare,
O'Ruark was absent—ah! would he were there;
Not then had Dearbhorgil forgotten her vows,
MacMurchad in triumph not borne off his spouse.
Throughout his dominions beloved and revered,
The brave Prince of Breffni by foemen was feared;
High feats of his prowess in arms have been told,
But little of this recked MacMurchad the bold.

Now quickly their steeds the O'Ruarks bestrode,
Some followed MacMurchad, to the monarch
    some rode,
And a faithful retainer soon hurried away
To relate to O'Ruark the deeds of the day,
Who from his devotions full quickly returns
To marshal his bands and march to the Ferns;

But the spies hovering round him his doings un-
    fold—
" Let him come with his clan," says MacMurchad
    the bold.

The King sent a courier to Leinster to say
MacMurchad should answer and not make delay,
Should give up his bride to O'Ruark again,
And make reparation most fully, in pain
Of the monarch's displeasure, who sought to re-
    strain
The lawless, licentious, and wished to maintain
Both morals and government pure as of old—
" I shall keep my young bride," says MacMurchad
    the bold.

At once to the rescue most willingly flew,
To aid brave O'Ruark, the pure and the true ;
The prayers of virtue ascended for him,
And husbands and fathers with anguish looked
    grim,
And Roderick, the King, with his followers came
And marched over Leinster with sword and with
    flame,

And now, as his army the allies enfold,
Fast flies from his country MacMurchad the bold.

To Henry of England the traitor now hies,
While O'Ruark is watched by retainers and spies,
And Henry soon granted the succor desired,
At once with the conquest of Erin inspired :
Though the King and O'Ruark are still in the
    field,
And justice is theirs, in the end they must yield,
For backed by his hirelings and flushed with his
    gold,
Returns to his country MacMurchad the bold.

It boots not to tell of the deeds that were done,
How freely the blood of the patriots run,
At last how dissensions their councils divide,
Forgotten was honor, and country, and pride,
How the banner of green at last trailed in the
    dust,
How base England triumphed, unrighteous, un-
    just,
How Ireland was conquered by treason and gold,
Dearbhorgil the frail and MacMurchad the bold.

Shaving.

 EAR after year brings changes in its
train,
But for the good old days we hope in
vain ;
Days ere the beard its " formal cut " received,
Days ere its loss incipient manhood grieved,
When flowing locks were honored as was due,
Tokens of age and marks of wisdom too ;
Whose growth luxuriant gave majestic air
To father Adam, first of human pair,
And pleased young Eve, who, innocent of guile,
Received her lover-husband with a smile,
Leaned on his arm with new and matchless
grace,
And laid her soft cheek to his whiskered face,
The nectar fit for gods presumed to sip,
And pressed her mouth on his unrazored lip ;
Whilst he her golden locks admiring twined,
To all the bliss of tender love resigned.

The downy cheek, o'erspread with blushes bright,
Was not a fairer picture in his sight
Than was to her the bold and manly face
Whose beard, soft flowing, was its crowning
      grace;
And thus distinct, yet perfect past compare,
Man's bearded strength and woman's beauty rare.

How long must we those halcyon days repine,
Ere razors scraped the "human face divine;"
Ere votive offerings, every morning made,
On heathen altars with deep groans were laid!
Oh blessed days! I sigh for your return,
When taste and fashion bade the beard be worn,
When men as yet were guileless of that sin,
And no shaved corner e'er revealed the chin;
Or, thus disgraced, his face he dare not show,
But tarried for his beard in Jericho.

Can blessings rest upon that wretch's head
Who first invented razors, and thus spread
Dire devastation over all mankind—
Unhappy race to such a fate consigned?
Of all the ills Pandora's box contained

Of which beard-growing mortals have com-
    plained ;
Of all the foul inventions which beset
Our path from youth to age, the foulest yet,
The worthiest of a mean half-bearded knave,
Is that seducing all the world to shave !

Oh ! that the blade which first his eyesight
    cheered
Had cut his throat instead of shaved his beard !
What mortal man whom fashion bids to shave
Would not rejoice to be no more a slave ?
For when the face its graceful garb had shed,
The razor next attacked the honored head ;
The flowing locks were strewn along the ground,
Grace, beauty, strength, no more on earth are
    found.
Thus false Delilah for great Samson spread
Snare upon snare, on whose devoted head
Large price was laid, but while his hair remained
Withes, cords, nor web his liberty restrained :
But once the razor touched his sacred head
His courage failed him and his vigor fled ;
His strength was gone, Delilah took the gold,

To base Philistines was brave Samson sold !
Then did this beardless, godless race rejoice,
And to great Dagon raise a thankful voice
That the dread foe into their hands was given
Who long for bearded Israelites had striven.
For years his limbs the fettered brass confined,
Poor blind old man to a hard fate consigned,
And not until his hair was grown again
Could he be found among the ranks of men ;
Then fully he avenged the treacherous plot
That brought him to that foul and hapless lot ;
And dying 'mid ten thousand dying foes,
His soul, superior over all, arose.
As rolling years with silver strew the head,
From which the raven curls of youth are fled,
The young with reverence view the hoary sage,
And gaze subdued upon the brow of age.
Thus do the locks that grace the human head
A constant beauty o'er the owner shed ;
So too the beard a manly mark displays
The sense and taste of men of ancient days—
Of men obedient to their Maker's laws,
Men unseduced, by every trivial cause,
To follow stranger gods' forbidden ways.

Thus age on age the sacred beard was worn ;
Men went, as Nature meant, with face unshorn,
But dressed with care, and trimmed with nicest
    art,
To please the fair and captivate the heart ;
Content and happy, nor intent to move
Upon Eternal Wisdom to improve.
Oh ! that mankind had kept his first estate,
Nor sought inventions out to change his fate !
Why should a beard spring from the manly face,
And aspect grave and look sedate invoke ;
And witching woman, infinite in grace,
Soft-lipped and tender-cheeked, our love pro-
    voke—
Save in obedience to some grand design,
Some law of Nature, lasting as divine ?
Who then against superior wisdom wars,
Or who in beauty shall his taste exalt ?
Shall man presume to think Omniscience errs,
And that which he calls "good" pronounce a
    fault ?

Then let the razor be the law no more ;
Let barefaced fashion's tyrant reign be o'er ;

Let each, by Nature bounteously supplied
With graceful beard, deem it a source of pride :
If worn with care it will the face adorn,
And no true woman will a whisker scorn.
So will the beard regain its ancient place
And give new beauty to each manly face,
Be the forerunner of a taste refined,
Incite to glorious deeds the waking mind.
No longer will the morning hour be spent
In groans, and tears, and face with soap besprent,
But graver cares discussion will invite,
And useful books to active life incite ;
And thus the mind, with daily food supplied,
Up, upward rises with a giant stride ;
Joys new and pure hence evermore will spring,
Exults the soul on her triumphant wing,
While every heart with emulation burns
And the lost golden age again returns.

Rowena.

A Historical Ballad.

THE subject of this ballad is an incident in the early history of England. The Romans, after having been masters of Britain nearly four hundred years, in the reign of the Emperor Valentinian, abandoned the island, having been rather forced to take this step, however, by the Picts and Scots, who were increasing in numbers in proportion as the forces of the Romans decreased. This was about the year of our Lord 447. The Britons, now left alone, were unable to defend themselves from the attacks of their Northern enemies, and fled for shelter to the woods and mountains.

In this deplorable state they had recourse to the Saxons, one of the most formidable of the nations of Germany. In consequence of the solemn invitation of Vortigern, who was at that time King of Britain, they, the Saxons, came to the assistance of the distressed islanders with a body of fifteen hundred men, under the command of two warlike brothers, Hengist and Horsa. The Saxons landed on the Isle of Thanet. The allies presently succeeded in driving their enemies beyond the borders of Britain. This was no sooner accomplished than the Saxons began to turn their own eyes toward the conquest of the rescued country. Accordingly a fresh supply of five thousand men, in seventeen vessels, passed over and succeeded in making a permanent establishment on the island. One of the reasons given by the British historians for the easy conquest of their country is the following, the subject of the ballad :

They allege that Vortigern was artfully inveigled into an attachment for Rowena, the daughter of Hengist, and in order to marry

her settled upon the father the fertile province of Kent, whence
the Saxons could never after be removed. It is added also that
upon another occasion, the weak monarch accepting of a festival
from Hengist, three hundred of his nobility were treacherously
slaughtered and himself detained as a captive.

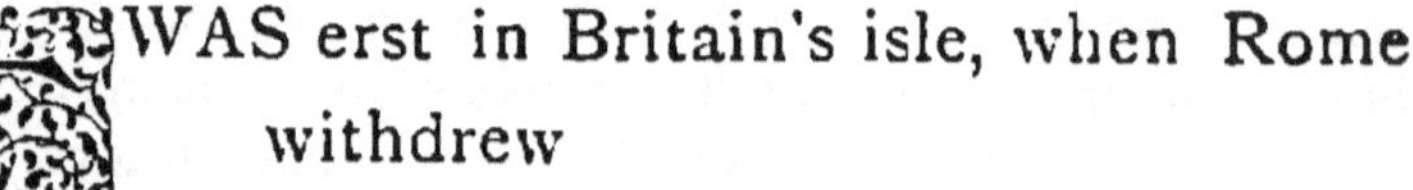

'TWAS erst in Britain's isle, when Rome
     withdrew
  Her conquering legions from its rocky
     shore,
That Northern Picts and Scots to battle flew,
Running with ruthless step the country o'er,
When horde on horde across the wall they pour,
And Britons fled for shelter to the caves
And woods and mountains, with their slender
     store ;
Driven by their foes they sank beneath the
     waves,
Or by the ocean back, they fell or lived as
     slaves.

At such a time, when every hope had fled,
And fell destruction hovered ever nigh,
A courier from the King full swiftly sped ;
He was a knight—of name and lineage high—

At dead of night the council bids him hie,
Clothed with authority in everything
The public good to aid, also whereby
He instant back unto his lord should bring
A band of arméd men from the old Saxon king.

Not many days—on Thanet's lovely isle
A band of arméd men was seen to land ;
The sight beguiles the Britons of a smile,
While warm they press the ready ally's hand ;
Nor long do they on ceremony stand,
The danger is too pressing—home and friends
And country the immediate care demand ;
For e'en to barbarous breasts this wish extends,
As with the roughest day a ray of sunshine
    blends.

And hand in hand where fiercest battle grows
The British and the Saxon soldier bled,
From field to field still headlong on their foes
They filled the land with hecatombs of dead ;
And Picts and Scots ingloriously have fled,
And peace comes smiling o'er the desolate
    plain.

The welcome news to Saxony has sped,
And princesses and maids, a comely train,
To celebrate the day, come gaily o'er the main.

A festival, a festival,
  The Saxon leader gives,
And British knights and nobles
  To his table well receives;
For the allies are triumphant,
  And northern hordes no more
Shall run the sunny hillside
  And the smiling valleys o'er;
The British king Vortigern,
  In magnificent array,
With regal pomp and train appears
  To solemnize the day,
The noblest of the noble;
  But the fairest of the fair
Is the Saxon maid Rowena,
  With blue eyes and golden hair.

When the herald loud announced him
  The Saxons all stood up;

In each hand, half raised in homage,
  Was a sparkling brimful cup ;
Hengist brought his noble daughter,
  Paying every homage due ;
And her high and brilliant beauty
  Soon the king's attention drew ;
Modestly the cup presenting,
  " Waes hael halford cyning,"
Said the maid in accents low ;
  And the king dreamed not of sinning
As he answered, " Drinc hael," bowing ;
  For the fairest of the fair
Was the Saxon maid Rowena,
  With blue eyes and golden hair.

Welcomed thus with wine and beauty,
  What could e'en a monarch do ?
Vain to talk of frigid duty,
  Gazing in those eyes of blue ;
Crown and kingdom won so lately,
  So much blood and treasure lost,
Now are worthless to Vortigern,
  On a sea of passion tost :
Deep he quaffed the wine-cup, deeper,

Till his senses seemed to reel ;
Gazing on that face angelic
    What a frenzy does he feel—
Planning what should win the favor
    Of the fairest of the fair,
The young Saxon maid Rowena,
    With blue eyes and golden hair.

Naught too foolish for a lover ;
    Off to Hengist straight he went,
Offering to him for his daughter,
    The rich vales of fertile Kent.
Quickly were espousals settled,
    For the chief was nothing loth,
And it wanted but the maiden
    Now to pledge her virgin troth ;
And would she refuse a kingdom,
    And a king of manly mien,
He a lover kneeling to her ?
    Such a thing was never seen,
And I trow it never will be ;
    So at once they both repair
To the Saxon maid Rowena,
    Who was fairest of the fair.

It was sunset--glorious sunset !
  Just the hour to lovers dear,
And the scene a rock close shaded,
  And a streamlet murmuring near,
Where the king and blue-eyed maiden
  Wandered a delightful hour,
All abandoned to the rapture
  Of their young love's witching power.
He had wooed the maid and won her,
  Had obtained her virgin vow,
He had kissed the lips so ruby,
  He had smoothed her snowy brow,
He had sworn to love her ever,
  And the ring he bids her wear
Proves the Saxon maid Rowena
  To be fairest of the fair.

Meanwhile boisterous is the frolic
  At the Saxon festival,
And the jovial song and laughter
  Echo through the spacious hall,
And the shades of evening darken,
  And the cup goes quickly round,
But the Saxons quaff not deeply ;

For the cunning Hengist found
Means to whisper his retainers
    That the British knights should die
While they yet suspected nothing
    And the merriment was high—
While the king was absent dallying
    With the maid of golden hair,
The beautiful Rowena,
    Long the fairest of the fair

Hark ! the angry steel is clashing.
    Where is Hengist, where the King?
Where Rowena's blue eye melting,
    Holds him in a magic ring ;
Hengist meets the happy lover
    As a father meets his son,
For he feels 'tis useless asking
    If the maiden has been won ;
For so fondly leant she on him,
    And so proudly trod the King,
That a stranger might have noted
    Some extraordinary thing
Gave to each so pleased an aspect;
    To the one a good-like air,

To the maid the palm, undoubted,
  Of the fairest of the fair.

Silence reigns where mirth presided
  But so lately in his glee,
And the hall with lights is gleaming—
  What a shocking sight to see!
Blood in streams from corpses flowing—
  Ghastly gashes gaping wide,
Groaning sufferers wildly praying
  Some to stop the gushing tide,
While another, scorning mercy,
  Opes the stanching wound anew ;
Hundred lights are weaving through them,
  Sure the work of death to do ;
Not a Briton had escaped them
  Had not instant entered there,
The King and Hengist and Rowena, .
  Fairest maiden of the fair.

All aghast stood King and chieftain,
  While Rowena shrieked in fright,
But the slaughter was suspended,
  Cared for every wounded knight.

As among his bleeding nobles
  Full of sorrow stood the King,
Wondering how again to friendship
  He those bitter foes could bring,
Straight before him stood bold Hengist.
  Pointing to the corpses strewn
O'er the hall in blood still weltering,
  Spake he in a solemn tone :
"Sire, our friendship needs cementing—
  Let us here allegiance swear ;
Wed thou our beloved daughter,
Young and noble, kind and fair."

No alternate was there left him.
  There surrounded by the dead
Were the King and well-born maiden
  By the holy Druid wed !
Ah ! it was a ghastly bridal !
  Gaudy trappings there were none ;
Over pale and bleeding followers
  Flickering torches faintly shone ;
Not a sound of gladness greets them,
  But a sadness is o'er all,
As respectfully they gather

Toward the centre of the hall ;
At the sacerdotal " Amen,"
    Every knight and noble there
Bows the knee and swears allegiance
    To the fairest of the fair.

Progress of the Age.

ONCE on a time, on Susquehanna's side,
Of all its denizens the joy and pride,
A smiling village rose, embowered in trees
That cooled the noon and wooed the evening breeze.
To which on gala days the youths repair,
Enjoy the Fourth, the muster, or the fair,
Bring to the sport strong limbs and healthy mind,
And manners warm if brusque and unrefined;
While all the village belles and beaux went out,
Joined in the sport, and swelled the joyous shout.

The country poured rich treasures at its feet;
The merchant sought but gain with justice meet;
For sale and barter still on hand had he
Silks, lawns, and muslins, coffee, pepper, tea;
So prospered each, each other's wants supplied,
And all with care their riches multiplied.
The doctor tried to heal instead of wound,

Each case was his for miles the country round ;
No golden-headed cane turns up his nose,
But kind and common through his world he
    goes.
If the vexed mind was cause of the disease,
The doctor's kindness gave it instant ease ;
If poverty with griping hand was there,
The doctor's larder answered to the prayer.

The parson too claimed brotherhood with all,
And warmly welcomed both the great and small.
The horny palm of laboring man would press,
And all his flock instinctively caress,
Visit them oft, their little sorrows share,
And soothe their passions with the words of
    prayer,
Know all their wants and many wants supply,
And when their joy was full, his kindling eye
And kindly voice directed them on high.

The lawyer too—the village boasted one—
Was fain to settle all disputes begun.
No pettifogging limb of law was he,
With pompous air and foreign pedigree,

To broadcloth, wine, and billiards early wed,
All on his back and nothing in his head :—
He was the friend of all who sought his aid,
And lived and died with conscience unbetrayed.
Such was the man—familiar but not rude—
To study given, but not to solitude—
Learned but no pedant—of a cheerful mind,
To chess and Greek, as well as law, inclined.
While oft the parson and the doctor sat
Till late at night enamoured of his chat,
The tradesmen and mechanics were no less
The friends and auditors his cheer could bless.

At dances, parties, picnics, routs, and shows,
Without distinction mingled belles and beaux
The sun-browned laborer was held no worse
Than he who had a thousand in his purse ;
The merchant flirted with the pretty maid
Who oft brought butter to the store to trade,
And the sweet daughter of our millionnaire
Danced with the blacksmith's son—a handsome
　　pair :
'Twas pure amusement all, and glee and song
Hurried on wings the precious time along ;

Dissatisfaction fled from every face,
And pleasure seemed the genius of the place.
Thus long we wandered, a benighted race,
Each one regardless of his proper place ;
We knew no better—be this our excuse
And shield our heads from well-deserved abuse ;
For other counsels rule our quiet town—
To see mechanics *now* we all look down ;
And some who oft together walked the street
No longer know each other when they meet.
Thus have we learned at last to strut, and stare
At well-known faces with an absent air,
And now can tell what quality of clay
A man is made of by the grand display
He makes of broadcloth, rings, et cetera.
Thank God ! each knows his place, and now we
    see
No rough mechanic at the dear *soiree*,
But gentlemen of standing, ladies fair ;
Bewhiskered city clerks with vacant stare,
Barbers disguised as counts, with foreign air
And most superior manners, here repair.
No noisy, mirthful crowd disturbs repose—
A few may whisper while the many doze ;

No songs, no vulgar laughter now are heard,
But languid smiles and simpers are preferred.
We shall improve, our teachers tell us, yet,
And soon become a quiet, genteel set,
Who of ourselves shall take a proper view,
Who know our rights, and will maintain them, too.

Heigh-ho!   I wish this progress had not come.
The "upper ten" you seldom find at home,
And if you do, each syllable they say
Is uttered in the most malicious way.
No kindly laugh disturbs the languid face,
But a half-sickly smile usurps its place,
And after chill half-hours among them spent,
You gladly leave, half sorry that you went ;
But sadder far to see enjoyment pall,
And cold convention freeze the mirth of all.

You dare not go among the "thousand" now—
'Twould stamp disgrace forever on your brow ;
A rough mechanic you would dare to treat
With only half a nod upon the street,
And to address a woman in a gown
Of calico would drive you from the town !

We do not meet as years ago we met,
Ripe for enjoyment, a promiscuous set ;
No ! no ! those days have fled—those halcyon
     days,
Worthy the gods and meet for poet's praise.
Mourn ! mourn ! ye youth ! the golden age is
     o'er,
And dances, routs, and picnics are no more.
A rough mechanic dares not now intrude
Upon a lawyer's sacred solitude,
And silks and satins are divinely pressed
By broadcloth sleeves against a satin vest.
Old things are done away ; behold, we view
Progress and change, but not improvement too."

Woe worth the day when caste and wealth shall
     be
The charms that pass to "good society ;"
Let laboring hands and thinking brains unite,
Each do its proper work with all its might ;
Nor gold nor silk shall pave the way to fame,
Nor honors gather round an ancient name.
Here every man shall act a glorious part
If sound in mind and of a loyal heart,

Unmindful if his father shaped the tool,
Or held the plough, or taught the village school,
Or to the parson's self was near allied :
Each his own stock shall in himself take pride.

Ode

FOR THE FOURTH OF JULY.

AGAIN has come the glorious day,
　　How blithe is every heart,
　　How splendid is the proud array,
　　It makes the life-blood start.
Now the brave veteran's sparkling eye
Brightens as in days gone by,
And once again he tells the tale
Which oft has turned his hearers pale,
And vivid paints before their eyes
The swift attack—the night surprise—
The lonely watch—the meagre fare—
Their hopes elate—their blank despair.

Tells of the carnage and the rout,
　　The slain where hosts had striven,
The vict'ry—the triumphant shout,
　　Whose pæan swelled to heaven ;
The bivouac—the social mess—

With glimpses faint of happiness ;
The cup—the patriotic song
That wiled the tedious time along ;
The soldier friend, the true, the brave,
Who now lies mould'ring in the grave ;
And as he names the friend once dear,
Pays him the tributary tear.

But now no more the trumpet horn
  Calls forth contending foes,
But yellow waving wheat is shorn
  Where bristling bayonets rose ;
Where charging squadrons reared and sprung,
And many a clanking sabre rung,
Where once the hardy foemen met
With glittering sword and bayonet,
Where horse and rider cold in death
Lay stretched upon the bloody heath,
Long since the waving grass has grown,
And flowers have wreathed each bleaching bone.

Hark to the rolling drum, and see,
  Borne lightly on the air,
The banner of the proud and free,

The banner bright and fair.
And now the cannon's deaf'ning roar
Again resounds from shore to shore,
And loud huzzas around arise
That fill the concave of the skies,
And many a tribute now is paid
To those whose heads are lowly laid,
And many a name is loudly rung,
And many a gallant deed is sung.

Yes! 'tis the great, the glorious Fourth!
   Rejoice! rejoice! rejoice!
Let East and West and South and North
   Raise a triumphant voice.
'Twas on this day our fathers broke
The British monarch's galling yoke,
It was this day that pealed on high
The first loud shout of victory,
And on this day the world beheld
A nation free, a cloud dispelled,
A little band of patriots rise—
A nation's pride and sacrifice.

How proud each freeman treads the sod!
  How fires his flashing eye !
And muttered praises to his God
  In patriot cheering die !
He thinks but on the gallant band
That stood the bulwark of the land,
And from the plains of Lexington
Till Washington at Yorktown won,
Follows again the bloody route,
Hears the low groan, the thrilling shout,
By grief and joy alternate swayed,
Till the last glorious charge is made.

How many names of high renown
  That page of early hist'ry shows—
Names which a wreath of honors crown
  Presented by both friends and foes.
Look for one moment o'er the scene :
There Warren comes with gallant Greene ;
With heavy guns and thundering knocks
The steady, earnest, honest Knox,
And pressing forward there we see
  Putnam and Morgan, Marion, Lee,
With many a soldier, many a sage
  Shed glory on that early page.

Let us enjoy without regret
  Spoils that the gallant dead have won ;
DeKalb, Pulaski, Lafayette,
  Steuben, and God-like Washington.
Spread out beneath a smiling sky
Millions on millions acres lie,
Won by the high-souled men who bore
The hardships of the fight of yore,
Whose names we celebrate to-day,
Whose deeds shall last till sun's decay,
While by their mother earth caressed,
On well-fought fields their ashes rest.

From the far snow-capped hills of Maine
  To Mexico's bright clime,
Rises on high a glorious strain—
  We're brothers for all time.
Let freedom's blessings spread abroad
The rights of man, the praise of God,
And bring within her hallowed fold
Each heart that's cast in manly mould,
Spreading her ægis o'er the whole,
From sea to sea, from pole to pole,
Till through the world's immensity
Man shall enjoy sweet liberty.

The Susquehanna.

 RIVER of the winding shore,
Could I but tell thy beauties o'er,
How many a stream that now, per-
chance,
Has high renown in old romance,
Or was, when yet the art was young,
In verse by ardent poet sung,
Should be eclipsed by thee !

The earth has nowhere greener fields
Than thy refreshing moisture yields ;
Though loftier mountains crown the Rhine,
None are more beautiful than thine ;
Health through thy fertile valleys roams,
And virtue blesses all their homes
With pure felicity.

Thy banks are rich with standing corn,
Thy golden wheat is still unshorn ;

In the sweet clover feed the kine,
Or in the oak's broad shade recline,
Until the milkmaid, blithely gay,
All redolent of new-mown hay,
    Comes tripping o'er the stile.

I love the breeze that sweeps thy hills;
Thy music, Susquehanna, fills
My soul with vast and pure delight;—
Whether thou glidest silv'ry bright,
Or, swollen with springtide rain and snow,
Thou pourest, with impetuous flow,
    Majestic to the sea.

Still queen of every native heart,
O! ever beauteous as thou art,
How far soe'er thy children roam
Thy valleys ever are their home,
Thy islets green seem ever near,
And ever sounding in their ear
    Thy murmuring melody.

I seek not Arno's shelvy side,
And bonny Doon shall ne'er divide

My steadfast heart and hope from thee ;
Among thy wildnesses I see
Unwritten romance—but, oh ! where
The wizard hand that now may dare
　　To start the forms to life ?

Oh ! would that I could bring once more
Van Campen to thy winding shore,
And o'er the hill at shut of day
Upon the war-path urge his way,
And make each creek and hillside rife
With war-whoop shrill, and sound of strife,
　　And deadly revelry ;

Re-people thy now peaceful shore
With bands as hostile as of yore,
Bring the wild chieftain of his race,
With eagle plume and painted face,
With tomahawk and bended bow,
And hundred warriors on his foe,
　　All eager for the fray ;

Paint the wild scenes among thy hills,
Along thy creeks and sparkling rills ;

Depict the hunt toward the lake,
The fight, the gauntlet, and the stake ;
What mighty deeds I might rehearse
In high and never dying verse,
    If Cooper's pen were mine!

The hope is vain. 'Tis not for me,
Weird Susquehanna, to set free
And clothe again in human mold
The shades that nightly stalk each wold,
And ere they pass beyond my ken
Wave over them the magic pen
    And bid them live for aye.

Mine is a less ambitious rôle ;
And though I oft at evening stroll
By old-time path across the hill,
And see the stalwart shadows steal
Athwart my way with noiseless tread,
I only wander, spirit-led,
    To muse, sweet stream, by thee.

To gaze upon the summits high
That thy unfailing source supply,

To wonder with what awful stroke
Thy waves thy mountain barrier broke,
To think how many thousand years,
Back to the ages of the seers,
    Thy history may run ;

How many thousand yet to come,
When all who know thee now are dumb,
Thy limpid stream will still run on,
Thy valleys glimmer in the sun,
Thy beauties chain the hearts of men,
Thy praise be chanted yet again,
    When I am all unknown !

Thy sparkling waters met my sight
When first my eyes beheld the light ;
And when at last I take my rest,
Then lightly on my sinking breast
I pray thy kindly loam may press,
And fold me in that long caress
    Which the last trump shall break.

Castle=Building.

WHEN eve has come, and in my lonely
room
I watch the sparkling fire the walls
illume,
Oft as I gaze my glowing fancy frames
Familiar forms and faces in the flames;
Reverting then to memory's ample page,
I count the days that tell my little age,
Dwell on each joyous scene of boyish years,
Which fleeting time but mellows and endears,
And feel again the exultant spirit bound,
And hear the merry laugh go gleeful round.
New faces rise as still the years run on,
Some older ones are dim, and some are gone.
Each in his turn, each in his proper sphere,
In memory's magic glass they all appear.

Here glide along in retrospective view
The stream and mill where my first breath I
drew,

On whose green banks full many an hour I
    played,
Or as an angler plied my barbarous trade ;
The apple-tree whose scented, golden fruit
Spangled the sward around its gnarléd root,
Where many an hour, on Indian Summer days,
The smoky mountain drew my earnest gaze.

Next comes the image of some school-boy face
    With all its train of incident and fun ;
Then the gruff-visaged master has a place,
With frown and ferule, and his tardy grace
    For truant school-boy, or a task undone.
Fields, forests, rivers—what a numerous throng
Of images those faces bring along !
Pleasant or painful, sorrowful or gay,
Still memory stores them in her cells away.

Now let me trace the future of my life,
With joy, with sorrow, with misfortune rife.
What fortune shall be mine? Shall e'er my
    name
Be wafted to the realms of glorious fame ?

Yes, I perceive the shadowings of things
Through the thick darkness which around them
    clings ;
I see the expectant crowd about me throng,
And list with rapture to my silvery tongue ;
I hear the shouts and the prolonged huzzas
With which they greet each patriotic phrase ;
I see the senate with attentive ear
Respect the counsel of my youthful year ;
The civic wreath is bound about my brow,—
Can I fall back into retirement now ?
Will not the nation claim me for its own,
Demand the service of her gifted son,
And cheer him on, a glorious race to run ?

Ah ! 'tis not there that pleasure is complete ;
More solid joys around the fireside meet.
The cheerful wife who keeps her happy place,
And yearly grows to more engaging grace,
Above whose brow appears, now here, now there,
The rich adornment of a silvery hair ;—
The romping boy who feels himself a man,
And acts Napoleon on a smaller plan ;
Who ranges round the room his toys and chairs,

And gives command with more than Murat's
　　airs ;—
The fair-haired girl with mild yet laughing eye,
O'er whom you fondly smile—profoundly sigh—
One hour with such were worth a thousand years
Of fame posthumous, which so fair appears.

And thou, my muse ! wouldst thou attend me still,
Thou gentlest soother of each earthly ill ?
Allied to thee, the heavens, the earth, the main,
Would all be empires subject to my reign ;
The roaring flood, the gently murmuring rill,
The fierce simoon, the breeze that sweeps the hill,
The waving forest, every shrub and flower.
By turns are given to my minstrel power !
Thou at whose shrine the great are proud to bow,
How blest were I with such a friend as thou.

Thus oft I muse when at the close of day
I sit me down to wile an hour away ;
Thus oft I build my castles in the air,
And deck them off with all things rich and rare
Then all at once the grand chimeras fade,
And low in dust are the bright fabrics laid.

Spirit Melody.

THE spirit said, "Sing," as I wandered
Alone by the babbling brook,
Whose music welled up as I pondered,
Entranced o'er some magical book;
The days glided by me unheeded,
Their coming no pleasure could bring,
For the day and the night which succeeded
Unceasingly whispered me, "Sing."

That voice was the first in the morning,—
It came with the sun o'er the hill,
It seemed like a spirit-land warning
Mysteriously working its will;
The wind bore that voice to me often,
It came with the zephyrs of spring,
Low breathing, "The best way to soften
The harshness of life is to sing."

It came in the cool breeze of noontide,
While nature was musing at rest;

Though deep silence reigned o'er the hillside,
  My ear with its music was blest ;
The notes of the birds, as they wended
  Away on the swift-speeding wing,
With the hum of the bright insect blended,
  And whispered me gently to " sing."

As comes a sweet love-tale at evening
  To the heart, it thrillingly came,
Still into my willing ear breathing
  Its story of greatness and fame :
I listened with joy, though I trembled,—
  It seemed the behest of a king ;
I doubted no more, nor dissembled,
  'Twas certain the voice bade me " sing."

When the stars in their beauty were pouring
  A silvery sheen o'er the night,
My soul, with that spirit-voice soaring,
  Was off in far regions of light :
Its music was in and around me,
  Pervading each visible thing ;
Like a low, distant echo it bound me,
  Repeating that mystic word, " Sing."

The song of the syren subdued me,—
   I boast no Ulyssean art,—
With all of itself it imbued me,
   Enshrining itself in my heart ;
With Fate I could struggle no longer,
   The air seemed with music to ring,
Each moment the soft voice grew stronger,
   Till it bade me, in thunder tones, "Sing."

I sang—but how lame was the metre !
   I sang—but how common the theme !
Oh, teach me some strain that is sweeter,
   And grant me pure poesy's dream.
Since now to thy mandate I bow me,
   Deign o'er me thy mantle to fling ;
With all of *thy* spirit endow me,—
   Enable me truly to "sing."

Euchre.

 LISTENED, one night, to a party at
    play
At a game they called euchre, both
    pleasant and gay ;
And the calls, when a hand had been dealt to
    each one,
Were "I pass," "Take it up," or "I play it alone,"
Or in a full tone that no man could resist
The partner called out to his chum, " I'll assist."

And when on this evening the gay and the young
Were having this game their amusements among,
I sat looking on, scarcely knowing a card,
And giving the players themselves my regard,
Till the tender emotion I could not resist,
But straight loved the girl who called out, "I'll
    assist."

And thus as the game, amid laughter and fun,
With varied successes continued to run,

I forgot who had euchred or failed in his play,—
Forgot to keep game, though the knife by me
    lay,
But believe me, old fellow, I never once missed
A smile of the maiden who said, " I'll assist."

Although I to years of discretion had come,—
Had reached the full measure of bachelordom,
When a button the less gave me little distress,
Nor in linen quite spotless expected to dress,—
Yet all specks from the neat little collar I missed
Of the charming young maiden who said, " I'll
    assist."

This life is a game much like euchre, I find,—
Can be made very social if so you're inclined ;
And I saw that the interest flagged with the
    tone
Of the fellow who bullied, " I'll play it alone ;"
While each in the game with new zest would en-
    list
When the sweet little maiden called out, " I'll as-
    sist."

And I wished in my heart that this girl would
    agree
To give, through my life, her assistance to me,
To strengthen my hand when I faltered or failed,
To lighten the burdens that sin has entailed
And just when to play the right card I had
    missed,
Come on with those words full of cheer, " I'll
    assist."

While thus I sat musing the party had gone,
The room was deserted,—" I played it alone ;"
But the silvery laugh of the maiden I heard
Float away on the air like the voice of a bird :
To follow and seek her I could not resist,—
I spoke, and she whispering said, " I'll assist."

Truth and Falsehood.

WHILE slow-paced Truth is binding
   Her sandals on her feet,
Fleet Falsehood, always ready,
   Has passed the crowded street,
Nor in her haste forgotten
   Her version to repeat
Of last night's cruel scandal,
   Of yesterday's defeat ;
And thereupon her helpers,
   Rolling this morsel sweet
Under their tongues, go telling
   The tale to all they meet,
Each something thereto adding
   To make the charge complete.

The telegraph is captured,
   The daily paper too,
To aid in the sensation
   And swell the great ado ;

No privacy is sacred,
　　And soon, to interview
The wretched, writhing victim,
　　And probe him through and through,
The importunate reporters
　　Besiege his chamber door,
And, like the croaking raven,
　　Will leave it nevermore
Until each prurient detail
　　Is conned and gloated o'er,
And every festering sorrow
　　Is opened to the core.

Then in the morning's issue,—
　　For so the papers choose,—
The public taste is feasted
　　With garbage from the stews ;
And there our sons and daughters
　　Are well informed, betimes,
Of bold and esoteric
　　Debauchery and crimes ;
And there exultant Falsehood,
　　Glossed with a little truth,

Descants upon each detail
  To unsuspecting youth.

O sacred Truth! I pray thee,
  With banner wide unfurled,
Come, haste thee, bind thy sandals,
  Stride forth into the world.
Send thou the lightning message,—
  Seize thou the printing press,—
And meet again with Mercy,
  And Peace, and Righteousness.
The world is weary waiting,—
  Say, shall it not rejoice
To hear amongst the discords
  The music of thy voice?
We know that thou art mighty,
  And that thou shalt prevail,—
Raise high thy sun-bright banner
  And let thy power avail :
Gather the few who love thee,
  Lead thou thyself the van ;
Be what thou wert intended,
  The shield and hope of man.

POEMS TO MARGARET.

Ode to my Flute.

OH, how I love at evening tide
    To steal away from haunts of men,
And by the murmuring streamlet's
    side,
  That wanders through the lovely glen,
To sit upon a rustic seat
  When all around is calm and still,
And list thy music, clear and sweet,
  Re-echoing from every hill.

The cricket stops his chirp to hear
  The silvery sweetness of thy tone ;
The breeze and streamlet wandering near
  Mingle their music with thine own.
But soon thy rivals of the wood
  Arouse them from the dreamy trance

Of summer sunlight solitude,
  And boldly to the test advance.

The blackbird sings his evening song
  As tint by tint the daylight fades,
And whippoorwills the sound prolong
  Till katydids rejoice the glades;
And while the night comes slowly down,
  And hillside noises still increase,
The babel of the distant town
  Seems to grow less, and less, and cease.

Now twilight insects take the wing,
  The fireflies, hovering, light the grove,
The tree-frog now essays to sing
  And deftly woes his lady-love;
And now, from every scented thorn,
  From every brake and bush and tree,
Upon the sighing breeze is borne
  A chorus of fierce melody.

O what a wild carouse we keep!
  How many noises crowd the air!
How many strains or loud or deep
  Or low or hoarse or faint or rare ·

And still beyond, and still beyond,
  Another and another note
Rolls with a penetrating sound
  From some new chaunter's throat.

All overpowered by nature's din,
  No more I breathe the silvery tone,
Nor hope the woodland praise to win
  While native minstrel pipes his own.
A thousand voices cheer the night—
  A thousand voices cry "encore,"
But thou and I, in fond delight,
  Disturb nor help the concert more.

Ode to the Wind.

THOU viewless Wind! mysterious thing!
From Southern vales I feel thee come,
And as thine unseen pinions wing
Their flight still North, the genial Spring
    Comes to our ice-bound home.
And while I sit and watch the star
    That ushers in the twilight hour,
And dream the maiden now afar
    Feels its magnetic power,
Thy gentle sigh, sweet Southern breeze,
    Is like to hers I love so well;
Then if I whisper 'neath these trees
    Wilt thou my message tell?
Sweet sighing Wind! bear to my Love
    The vows I breathe, the wish I make:
At twilight through her garden rove,
    Let her from thee my kisses take.

When stern November russets all the plain,
  And sweeping down o'er lake and fell,
  Of winter nigh thou seem'st to tell,
And the dark blustery night sets in amain ;
    By dying fire,
    My rustic lyre
The harp Æolian in the window strung,
    I much admire
    Thy fairy choir
That makes its music gently swell,
Whilst thou are breathing its charmed chords
  among
Such dulcet strains as erst the angels sung.

  Whence comest thou, mysterious thing ?
  Thy melody whence dost thou bring ?
  Thy chords are true to every sound
  In the enchanted circle found
   That music calls its own ;
  First wailing low like requiem sad,
  Then quick the merry notes and glad,
  Now distant far, then nearer by,
  Or sweet and low, or loud and high,
    Thy ever-changing tone.

While round the house with moaning wild
I hear thee rove,—once more a child,
I look toward my mother's chair,
Fearing the witches in the air,
And for a moment inly dread
The hour that strikes the time for bed.

The Northern gates are open wide,
And Boreas comes, with giant stride,
    With all his horrors at his back,
Fierce blustering through the air,
    Leaving destruction in his track,
And strewing riches rare
    Among the caves of ocean wild,
    Whilst continents are rudely piled
With works e'en time would spare.
Roaring and raging o'er the earth,
And laughing hoarsely in his mirth,
    The howling Wind sweeps by:
No music charms the listening ear,
    No gentle lullaby;
He fiercely howls and loudly roars,
    And hoarse and harsh the notes he pours,
A requiem to the parting year.

Blow, then, black Boreas ! from thy cave
Unchain the storms and let them rave ;
Tear from their homes the ancient trees ;
Show to the earth and foaming seas
The might reposing in thy breath,—
That to resist thy course is death.
Oh, how my soul delights to be
Alone with earth, and night, and thee.
On darkening storms of Winter tide
Grim and secure thy henchmen ride ;
O'er all the earth, with lordly reign,
O'er man, and beast, and mighty main,
Rude Boreas rules, dark, drear, and dread,—
The world is dumb and nature dead.

Parting.

Written on a Sleepless Night.

HY should we part? I know I dare
not love thee,
And yet thy spirit is akin to mine ;
Oh, may the sky be ever bright above
thee,
And sweetest flowers round thy pathway twine,
When we shall part.

Why should we part? I fear thou dost not love
me,
Yet very often doth thine eye meet mine ;
No other glance has half the power to move me,—
In sooth, I ask no answering eye but thine,
Why should we part?

Why should we part? Earth hath no dearer
pleasure
Than still to meet as we have often met ;

Like the old miser gloating o'er his treasure,
  Those moments we will hoard and ne'er for-
    get,—
              Though we shall part.

Why should we part? The nights will be so
    lonely
  When I no longer hear thy sweet, sad tone ;
For in the crowd that round us sat, thou only
  Could'st charm my ear,—I worshipped thee
    alone :
              Why should we part ?

Why should we part? We cannot meet another
  So prompt to understand the wayward heart ;
A sister's love, a kind protecting brother
  May not prevent regret's sad tear to start,—
              Why should we part?

But we must part ! And yet we fondly linger,
  We scarce know why, round each familiar spot
Where we can trace the print of mem'ry's finger
  And read a story ne'er to be forgot,—
              Though we must part.

Yes, we must part !   Regrets are unavailing,
   Yet will the mind oft on these meetings dwell ;
Our friendship and our love will be unfailing,
   Though we are forced at last to say "Fare-
     well,"—
             For we must part !

Noctes Ambrosiæ.

HE comes to - night!   The moments
strangely linger,
The sun yet lags above the distant
hill,
The clock scarce seems to move its laggard finger,
The shadow on the dial-plate stands still,—
He comes to-night.

He comes to-night!   At last the sun is sinking,
The shadows lengthen o'er the level plain ;
I grow impatient, gazing thus and thinking,
And waiting for his coming step in vain,—
He comes to-night.

He comes to-night!   The evening star is shining,
How can he loiter thus along the way ?
He knows that for his presence I am pining,
And chide the lazy hours of lagging day,—
He comes to-night.

He comes to-night!   And yet he is delaying,—
  My lips are burning for his cooling kiss ;
If I were he I would not thus be staying,
  And losing time so dear to love as this,—
                    He comes to-night.

He comes to-night!   I'll dream that he is present
  And closely folding me in mute caress ;
O ! thus to nestle in his arms is pleasant,
  And lip to lip in murmuring transport press,—
                    He comes to-night.

He comes to-night!   I feel his dear hand playing
  Among the flowing tresses of my hair,
While o'er my brow caressingly 'tis straying,
  Smoothing the locks that cluster thickly there,—
                    He comes to-night.

He comes to-night !   His gentle whisper, telling
  How dear he holds me in his inmost heart,
Falls thrillingly upon my ear, compelling
  The joyous tear-drops from my eyes to start,—
                    He comes to-night.

He comes to-night! How sweet to thus be
    dreaming,
  Imagining the bliss that he will bring ;
Hark ! 'tis his step ! no more my joy is seeming ;
  Now will the hours their course like lightning
    wing,—

        He comes to-night.

The Signal Lamp.

OWEVER murk the coming night,
  Thy window shows a constant ray,
And not the sun in beauty bright,
  When first he brings the rising day,
So thrills me as that taper-light.

Half hidden by that friendly tree,
  Its steady gleam still speeding far
Into the gloom that love may see,
  By thoughtless traveller deemed a star,
Tells me thou waitest then for me.

With silent step the trysting-place
  Beneath the low-grown pine I seek,
And scarcely wait a moment's space
  Till turret clock the hour bespeak
That brings thee to my arms apace.

O silent night ! O moonless sky !
  O hour that brings my Love to me !

More swiftly let each other fly,—
   I care not how the moments flee
That bring the one for which I sigh.

My sweetest, dearest, kindest, best,
   Thy love exalts my drooping heart ,
'Tis inspiration to my breast,
   And thy pure spirit doth impart
To mine a sense of peace and rest.

Kiss me, my Life : my spirit soars
   With thine in happy thoughts away,
While love o'er every action pours
   The radiance of the perfect day,
And youth, and all its hopes, restores.

Ah, youth ! if only thou couldst know
   And read the silent Fates aright,
How happy would our ages flow,
   Crowded with bliss of faith and sight,
Uncankered or by care or woe.

But 'tis not so ; and thus an hour
   Snatched from the care and toil of life

Within thy arms, hath greater power
    To fit me for the manly strife
Than fame and gold which souls devour.

Press dewy kisses on my mouth,
    And let me dream the night away ;
Think how my soul hath felt a drouth,
    Unwatered for this many a day
By balmy showers from the South.

Now let them come, borne on the sighs
    Of thy sweet breath, nor let them be
Cut by thy pearly teeth ; thine eyes
    Glancing meanwhile in mine, to see
The depths from whence my love doth rise.

Look in my heart, and thou shalt see
    A passion, pure as any flame
That burns on vestal altar free,
    Forever and for aye the same,—
A monument to love and thee.

Thy voice is music ; ay, thy feet,
    That press the sward so daintily,

To me make music exquisite,
　　Tripping toward the fragrant tree
Beneath whose sheltering boughs we meet.

I feel thy ringlets on my cheek ;
　　I touch thy hand,—O thrilling touch !—
I scarce can breathe, I cannot speak ;
　　The joy it gives is all too much
A foretaste of the bliss I seek.

Go on, gay world, in pomp and pride,
　　Who will, let him thy lucre share ;
I crave no other wealth beside
　　Thy love, a wealth beyond compare,
My own, my own, my spirit bride.

Waiting.

THE clock strikes ten! O weary, weary
    night,
  I watch and watch, no light thy win-
    dow shows,
'Tis darkness all, nor moon nor stars give light,
  The whistling wind mocks at my nightly woes,
I wait in vain, thou wilt not come again,—
O weary, weary night, the clock strikes ten.

A star might fall from heaven, and who would
    miss
  Its beams among the thousands yet on high?
I look not for it; my supremest bliss,
  That bliss for which I ever look and sigh,
Is the bright taper in thy window, when
In the old village church the clock strikes ten.

But though it strikes thou comest not, my Heart;
  I wait and wait, although I know full well

Thou wilt not come, yet can I not depart :
　Thoughts of the past hold me as in a spell.
I tell myself again and still again,
Yes, she will come ; wait till the clock strikes ten.

But the moon rises o'er the distant hill,
　I see it gleaming on thy window-pane ;
Down in the village every noise grows still,
　The lights fade out, darkness and silence reign ;
The measured stroke glides o'er the sleepy glen
Of sullen-sounding clock striking the hour of ten.

But when again that signal I shall see,
　How madly happy will that moment prove ;
Then will I meet thee at our favorite tree,
　And kisses mixed with murmured words of love
Fill up the night with joyful moments, when
Thy longed-for dainty step comes with the stroke
　　of ten.

Reality and Romance.

MAGGIE says I do not love her :
  Could the little witch discover
  How, when waking, each emotion
  Rises from the boundless ocean
Of my adoration deep,
Surely, thus her spirit longing
Would not, e'en in thought, be wronging
Or the passion which enthralls me,
Or the power which ever calls me
  To her, waking or asleep.

Maggie says I do not love her :
Could the little witch discover
How the midnight lamp is glowing,
All the classic lore bestowing
  On my mind for her dear sake,
She would glory that her power,
Like a constant, gentle shower,

Blesses still and makes me better,
And more worthy, when I get her,
    Her true happiness to make.

Maggie says I do not love her :
Could the little witch discover
How my heart and soul are growing
Through the blessing which is flowing
    From her spirit pure to mine ;—
How a high ambition urges
Me to battle with the surges
Which o'erwhelm the man who never
Was aroused to great endeavor
    By a love so strong as mine ;—

How each dormant sense is waking,
And its long-forged fetters breaking ;—
How each fibre of my being
Thrills with but the bliss of seeing
    Her lithe figure o'er the way ;—
How to me is soul-entrancing
Her bright eye, demurely glancing
Toward me, even though not meeting
Mine for e'en a moment's greeting
    In the glare of tell-tale day ;—

How her smile the future brightens,
How her love each labor lightens,—
Could she half of this discover,
All her fears would then be over
　　And her doubting heart at rest:
She should have the choicest blessing,
The most passionate caressing;
Of the very dearest blisses,
Of the very sweetest kisses,
　　Hers should be the very best.

Maggie says I do not love her:
Could the little witch discover
How the castles I am building,
With their carving and their gilding
　　Quaint and curious as of yore;
With their quiet, deep recesses,
Fitted well for sweet caresses,
Hung about with damask curtain,
Making light and shade uncertain
　　From the ceiling to the floor;

Filled with books of ancient learning,
Tales of lovers nightly yearning

For a smile to ease the sorrow
Still returning with each morrow
 Till the sweet probation's done ;
And among the pictures many,
She herself, more fair than any,
Sweeter far than any story
Told by harper old and hoary
 Since tale-telling was begun ;

How the walks and shaded bowers,
Redolent with sweetest flowers,
By the limpid streamlet winding
From the glare of sunlight blinding
 To the cool, dark cypress grove,
Where the birds are ever twittering,
And the far cascade is glittering,
To its noonday-twilight cover
Woos the maiden and her lover,
 With their new old tale of love ;

And that in that shaded bower
There is not so fair a flower ;
That her eyes are far more blinding
Than the sparkling water winding
 To the river deep and still ;

That her voice is far more cheering
Than the song of birds careering,—
Could she all these things discover,
She would surely know I love her
  With my very strongest will.

The Reason Why.

WHY do you love me? said my blushing
maid,
As on her head caressingly I laid
The sun-browned hand that wins my
daily bread;
It cannot be my wealth of golden hair,
For many maidens may with me compare
And this great crowning glory with me share.

Why do you love me?   Are my sweet gray eyes,
As you so often call them, such a prize
That, if they shone on you, you could despise
Golconda's gems and India's fields of gold?
Ah! these would give you happiness untold;
And ease from toil and care when years grow old.

Why do you love me?   I've no lily hand
With jewels decked.   One simple band
Of virgin gold is all it may command;

And though it thrills to the full finger ends
At clasp of yours, I cannot think it sends
Such transport through you as your tongue pre-
    tends.

Why do you love me?   I can never bring
To your acceptance any offering,
Great name, nor high estate, nor anything ;
I'm but myself and cannot, cannot guess
Why you should love me,—you, who might caress
The highest in the land.   I cannot, cannot guess.

Why do I love thee ?   It is nought to me
That high estates are wanting unto thee,
That jewels flash not o'er thee brilliantly,
Mere dross are they.   One living, golden hair
Is worth them all.   Thou art thyself, my Fair,
Made precious by thy love, thy heart a jewel rare.

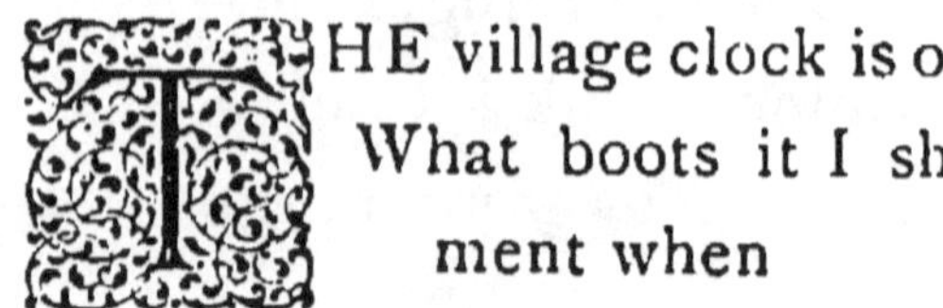 Ten O'Clock.

HE village clock is on the stroke of ten !
What boots it I should wait the mo-
ment when
Comes the glad hour I was to think of
thee ?
Sweet thoughts of thee are ever in my mind :
Would I could turn them into murmured words
And whisper them into thy willing ear,
And see thy cheek flush, and the half-formed tear
Moisten thine eyelid as it closed in joy.
It may not be !   Thought is my only bliss :
The sweet caress, the ripe and luscious kiss
Are mine no more, save in my happy dreams ;
From them I wake in ecstasy, to find,
Oh, sad reverse ! that I am all alone.
And thus I pass the livelong summer day,
Thus in uneasy sleep toss through the night,
Finding each morning thou art still away,
Until the yearning wish to see thy face,

To hear the music of thy cheery voice,
To twine my fingers in thy silken hair,
To bask and live within thy sunny eyes,
And feel about me thy sweet influence,
Grows agonizing in its vehemence.
Would I were with thee, for my earthly rest
Is only perfect pillowed on thy breast.

The Delayed Letter.

MY books lie dusty on the shelves,
The poets even charm no more ;
And as the days succeed themselves,
I idly sit, and wait, and wait,
Until I hear the rush and roar
Of iron steed, at rapid gait,
From sunset land come thundering :
Then follow, with impatient step,
The lazy postman to his goal,
And watch, in agony of soul,
As all too slowly, one by one,
The letters pass his curious gaze,
As if he stood there wondering
And all forgetful of his place :
And when at last the tale is done,
And all the waiters forward press,
He turns, with eye emotionless,
Upon me quickly striding through

The watching crowd, and answering
My eager look, for voice there's none,
In calm and even monotone,
He only says, " There's none for you."

The Magic Name.

OH that my pen, no longer roughly halting
  As heretofore on themes of common fame,
Now, when thy goodliness I am exalting,
  May write full gracefully thy magic name :
No longer painfully and slowly going,
  But tipt with words of sweetness and of truth,
That, from its diamond point full swiftly flowing
  Shall keep thy memory in perpetual youth.

Oh, fairer than the daughters of the morning !
  My heart is tangled in thy silken hair,
For thy sweet sake all other maidens scorning,
  Round thy dear name weaving sweet fancies rare.

See how each face grows brighter at thy coming ;
  Thine eyes with light divine my spirit bless ;

Thy lips are full of grace and ever charming,
  Oh, could I meet them in one long caress,
Or rest my head upon thy bosom, beating
  But one pulse faster for its being there,
Then might time fly; I would not stay its
    fleeting,
  Nor ask of other worldly bliss to share.
Fragrant as spring I catch thy gentle breathing,
  Less sweet the hawthorn scents the evening
    air ;
Thy garments smell of myrrh, aloes, and cassia,
  Thy person has a savor sweet and rare.

My days and nights are passed in pleasant
    dreaming
  Of that blest hour when I shall dream with
    thee,
Thy silk-brown hair around my pillow streaming,
  Thy ripe, crisp kisses unrestrained and free.
And yet it may be that best earthly blessing,
  With all my longing, never may be mine ;
But life itself were scarcely worth possessing
  If that dear hope and thee I must resign.

But I *do* know the time is surely coming
  When I shall clasp thee to my joyful breast,—
When, neither heart nor spirit longer roaming,
  I shall sit down with thee to love and rest.

Time.

LAZY, lagging Time !
When longing lovers wait a coming
    day
Thy chariot wheels stand still on
    Gibeon,
The moon waits o'er the vale of Ajalon,
Or on the dial the recording shade,
With reverse action, multiplies the hours.

So to my urgent thought this day appears.

How long the sun bides in the western sky !
Surely he hangs entangled in those clouds,
Enamored of the beauties they display !
See how they blush as he sinks into them
And draws the fleecy curtains round his form.

Thus the fresh bride, wrapped in her snowy
    robes,
With face half hidden by her golden hair,

On the first evening of the nuptial rite,
With brilliant blush and palpitating breast,
Meets the warm gaze and passionate caress
Of him, the day-god of her waking dreams.

Sink, laggard sun, and bring the blissful hour !

I beat the greensward with impatient foot,
And champing on his bit my neighing steed,
Ready an hour before 'tis time to start,
With pawing hoof chides my unused delay.

That maiden blush is still upon the clouds,
Less warm, less brilliant than an hour agone,
And fades, ah ! fades into the cold and gray !

But if the sun the God of Love should stay
The rosy hue would never pass away,
And life itself would wear e'en such a face
As the clouds wore but now a little space.

At last the shadow of the poplar tree
Marks the glad hour, and now we must be gone ;
The fancies of the hour will soon be facts,
And fleecy robes, and crimson glowing cheeks,

And golden hair, and breathings odorous,
And warm embraces will at last be mine,
    O lazy, lagging Time!

    O swiftly gliding Time!
Is it the sun that streaks the eastern sky?
'Tis scarce an hour since that the sun went down.
Indeed, methinks it must be but the glow
Of the departing day along the West
That streaks the eastern sky with faintest pink,
Or from the North perchance the ruddy shaft,
Shooting toward the zenith, brightens thus
Those clouds that rest upon the mountain tops.
    So let us sleep, the day will come anon;
It is enough we meet it when it comes.
Has it then come? Ay, Phœbus' morning kiss
Brings the bright blush to sweet Aurora's cheek,
But when I glance into those eyes of thine,
Thy deeper crimson shows Aurora pale.
    Then let us up, and on the ebb sea-shore
Gather of shells the livelong summer day.
Surely the yesterday that was so long
Cannot be followed by a brief to-day,
So let us sport the creeping hours away.

But so it was ; night came ere we began
To know our own capacities for bliss,
And thus day after day, year after year
Slipped by,—enjoyment lost for want of thought
Seeking beyond what lay within our grasp,
We let the golden moments pass us by
Till Time dashed down the cup whence we had
     quaffed
So many drafts of unconsidered bliss,
That with a sudden cry and start we wake
As from a dream, and mirrored we behold
The crow's-feet clustering about the brow,
The gray hairs mingled with the locks of jet,
The sunset clouds glowing along the West,
But with a tint less bright and beautiful
Than that which brought such hopes and visions
     dear
But yesterday,—what said I ?   Yesterday ?
And sighing deep, exclaim with sad surprise
O'er retrospect of many a vanished year,
     O swiftly gliding Time !

OUR JEWELS.

Our Baby Kate.

OUR baby Kate, lent to us for a while,—
Herself unconscious of the bliss she brought
And all unconscious of the ruin wrought,—
To cheer and gladden with her angel smile,
The hours unclaimed by labor stern to wile,
To open long-sealed springs of love and thought,
To teach us wisdom though herself untaught,
And lead at last to God our hearts so vile.
Lost to us here within the silent tomb,
But resting peacefully along with them
Of whom, 'tis said, they happy are that die:
A bud transferred from earth in heaven to bloom,
A shoot just starting from the parent stem,
A babe below on earth, a cherub in the sky.

Helen.

AND Helen too! sweet bud of early June,
Blessing our household but for three short years
With her dear face, her joys, her hopes, her fears,
Then parting from us sudden and so soon,—
Scarce three short days.   O! we did importune
High Heaven, that every supplication hears,
To grant our darling cherub to our tears :
But it was not to be.   Called to commune
Once more with death and view the silent tomb,
We laid our sweet babe in the quiet earth.
We did not seem to shudder at the gloom,—
'Tis but the passage to a glorious birth,
And lifting heart and faith, the Christian eye
Sees one more angel in the radiant sky.

Hope.

ONCE more, grim Death? Our boy,
our only one!
Couldst thou not spare us him? A
few short days
And thou didst bear along thy silent ways
A daughter,—now our darling Hope, our son!
Why should I now ambition's circuit run?
What now to me is wealth, or fame, or praise?
The loss of him all things like these outweighs.
My boy! my boy! My active life is done.
How sweet a tie are children to us here!
But when the Saviour calls them to His home,
Snapping the bands that keep our hearts below,
How longingly our spirits vault and go
With them, again in joyous group to roam,
Knowing and known beyond this mortal sphere.

 ND after years had fled, to bless our
          sight
       Another boy was given to fill our
          hearts,
Widen our sympathies, and heal our smarts.
Then labor had an object and delight;
Our "forward looking thoughts" discern no
    night;
Boyd takes the place left vacant, and imparts
To our dull household pristine joys and starts
Anew life's current, circling to the light :—
Death dashed our hopes to earth,—our dimming
    eyes,
And steps irregular, and wasting powers
Count years and days no longer, but count
    hours ;
And save one daughter dear, with winning ways
To brighten yet our fast declining days,
All our true treasures are laid up in Paradise.

Maude.

O THOU freed spirit, clothed in robes of
    light,
Our daughter Maude, ...
When we shall look into thy loving
    eyes,
Then faith and hope shall be eclipsed by sight :
O Death ! that lovest best what is most bright,
That still art deaf to all our prayers and sighs,
Thou with our daughter dost enrich the skies,
But leavest us poor and clothed upon with night.
The morning of her days was not yet spent,
No cloud seemed rising o'er her coming years,
And loving hearts and hands were by her side ;
And yet before we knew the shaft was sent,
Day darkened, and the tempest of our tears
Has no surcease,—sorrows with us abide.

One More Year.

ONLY a year had fled on silent wing ;
    The tears of sorrow had not ceased to
      flow :—
    The emptiness of heart, the sense of
      woe,
The longing which a chord of song will bring,
Of song which she, now absent, used to sing
    With rising note which set the heart aglow,
    The lightsome footstep coming swift and low,
The rustling garment, yet seemed lingering,—
    When he, a noble youth who held her pledge,
    Was called to go and seek her loving heart
In the sweet rest of sinless Paradise :
    With his deep-mourning mother to the edge
    Of the still, painless grave we went, to part,
But meet again our loved ones when the morn
    doth rise.

The End.

 MAUDE ! could I but come to thee
Where glows thy brilliant star,
Full well I know that I should be
Where the best and purest are.

MISCELLANEOUS.

Battle of Lake Erie.

SEPTEMBER 10, 1813.

" WHAT ! will they sweep the channels
And brave us as they go ?
There's no place in English annals
For the triumph of a foe."
—ADMIRAL BLAKE : *Poems of* L. E. L.

NO longer can that boast be sung ;
Haughty Britain now must know
There *is* "place in English annals
For the triumph of a foe."

Other fleets are on the ocean,
Other keels the waters lave,
And no longer can the sailor
Sing "Britannia rules the waves.'

In the West a nation rises,—
Hail, America ! to thee

All the world with hope is looking :
  God defend thy liberty.

Long shall Erie be remembered
  By the brave, a hallowed spot ;
For there Perry fought and conquered,—
  He nor it shall be forgot.

Bright the morning, bracing breezes
  Curled the foaming breakers high,
When proud Barclay, anchor weighing,
  Let the British streamer fly.

Quickly Perry calls to quarters ;
  Gallant tars with pleasure hear
Breezes through the rigging whistling,
  And the orders ringing clear.

Hark the conflict ! cannon flashing
  Lurid through the thick'ning smoke,
And the shivering masts are crashing,
  As if by a thunder-stroke.

Hotter, fiercer grows the battle,
  Closer, closer gun to gun ;
Not a man in all the squadron
  Seeks a sailor's death to shun.

Bared each breast, each eyeball glaring,
  Face begrimed with smoke and blood,
Nothing but dishonor fearing,
  To his work each seaman stood.

Pouring broadside after broadside
  Fiercely home upon the foe,
Till their decks, so great the slaughter,
  With a crimson current flow.

See brave Perry, in the battle
  Leave the Lawrence flagship side,
And upon the foaming water
  'Mid a thousand bullets ride,—

Bring the fleet to closer action,
  Pour its storm upon the foe,
Till first one and then another
  British pennon was laid low.

It is done : Trafalgar cannot
  Boast a brighter wreath of flowers,
And thus Perry told the story :—
  "We have met, and they are ours."

The Knight of St. John.

ND long and bold we fought the Turk.
And, Adrian, it was knightly work,
When, slow and deep, the lines ad-
vance
To charge upon them with the lance,
To hear the dogs to *Allah* cry,
And in the very shout to die.
But truth was on the Christian's side
And gave his arm its wondrous power,
Full often stemmed the battle's tide,
And turned the fortune of the hour.
Ah! yes, it was a splendid sight,
To see us charge their camps at night;
Stealthily first, then with a yell
Which roused the nodding sentinel,
Who never rose from where he fell.
But when the clashing steel is heard,
Then shrilly rings the rallying-word,
The captains start, and everywhere
Gleams forth the Turkish cimeter;

The alarm,—the quick retreat,—the chase,—
Christian and Turk in heady race,
And the whole plain in uproar wild,
Foeman and friend together piled ;
The loud command, the sweeping charge,
The shouts of triumph, groans of pain,
Which o'er the field are heard at large,
Now fiercely loud, now low again !
On every side great deeds were done,
Each knight his battle lost or won :
Here breaks a lance with quivering crash,
And here the gleaming sabres flash ;
Here, at a sweeping gallop, come
The Turks, and here the knights charge home ;
While o'er the plain full many a steed
Bounds wildly, from his rider freed,
And with fierce neigh of rage or pain
Joins the embattled host again.
And now, as every sword is out,
The Templars, with their battle-shout,
Bear fiercely down upon the foe,
Whose turbaned ranks with fury glow,
Till far along is heard the tramp
Of rushing steeds from the farthest camp ;

They come ! they come ! and swift and strong
The increasing numbers pour along ;
Then one last charge to check their pride,
And slowly back the Christians ride.
With short repose from midnight fray
Prepare for strife the coming day,
Or under flag, with pallid cheek,
The brother, friend, companion seek,
And with hot tears, at evening pay
The last sad honors to his clay.

A Valentine.

O BLESSED saint! O sweet Saint Val-
    entine!
To-morrow, yes, to-morrow is thy
    day:
Then will the birds warble sweet roundelay,
And cooing bills with cooing bills entwine:
Then will the earth send up the clinging vine,
Making sweet promise to the budding May
Of leaves of living green and flowers gay
And shady groves and days of auld lang syne:
Are those old days by thee forgotten quite?
Quite unforgotten are those days by me—
Quite unforgotten is the starless night,
The sweet-breathed murmur of the low pine
    tree,
The thrilling touch of lips, the sweet delight
Of the sweet moment that I stood by thee.

A Remembrance.

WHY should I send a Valentine to greet
One who forgets now those delicious
    days
    When Cupid met us at the cool cross-
    ways,
Picking of berries by the hedges sweet;
While ever and anon our hands would meet
Where the ripe fruit loaded the bending sprays,
When her shy eyes would droop beneath my
    gaze,
And rose and lily on her cheeks compete?
She may not wish those idlings to recall :
May be Young Love, yet to itself unknown,
Came to her as a fond delicious dream
From which she has not waked—leave her in
    thrall
Until her heart bounds to the trumpet tone
Of Love full grown—she will my heart redeem !

Unforgotten.

WITH what a full and infinite delight
Some things remain upon the mem-
    ory !
    All else may wander on the wild, wild
    sea,—
This, hidden in some chamber out of sight,
Remains forever pure, forever bright.
So if thou shouldst at last forgetful be,
Nor bear me longer in thy memory,
And as the winter days take their dull flight,
Give me no token, bar me from thy sight,
Leave me as restless as the wild, wild sea,
Hoping, but getting not one word from thee,—
Still unforgotten be that starless night
When, as we stood beneath the shadowing pine,
I for one moment pressed my thrice-blest lips
    to thine.

The Bee.

'VE wandered with the Bee to-day
  By many a modest flower,
On many a grassy bank at play,
  For many an idle hour ;
Have watched it seeking honey-dew
  From morn till evening gray,
From blooms of every scent and hue,
  This happy, happy day.

Then, laden with the golden sweet,
  On tireless wing it flew,
And left me by the mossy seat
  Alone with thoughts of you ;
Thoughts sweet as blossom to the shower,
  As twilight to the day,
Which drew me to your fairy bower,
  Upon that evening gray.

And there the Bee was lingering too,
  Full loth to go away,—

Unmindful of the falling dew,
  And of the evening gray ;
Why chide the nectar-sipping bee,
  Forgetful of the hours ;
The midnight star observed that we
  Were kissing 'mongst the flowers.

With an Inkstand.

Y dear Puss! I declare
If I had been aware
That this wedding of yours
Was to happen this fall,
My devotion to you,
So deep and so true,
Would have bid me to seek
Some remembrance unique,
That would serve to recall,
When away from us all,
Some hours of the past
Much too happy to last.

But no time to prepare—
Not a moment to spare ;
And the summary way,
On this short autumn day,
That you leave us all here,
In this northern sphere,
To the cold and the blast,

While you speed away fast
To the land of the sun,
And the orange and lime,
Just gives me a shiver
Clear down to the liver,
Where the Greeks used to say
That the seat of love lay.

My thought, and my duty
To love and to you,
Was at once to devise,
For the light of your eyes,
To mark each bright hour
In your charming boudoir,
A time-piece of beauty
In a silver horseshoe !

But this, my design,
Was so out of the line
Of the jeweller's thought
That it had not been wrought,
And could not be got.

Therefore this antique,
But not very unique
Piece of bronze I present,
By the jeweller sent.

While it is, of a truth,
Not a fountain of youth,
Upon whose mossy brink
You are lingering to-day,
To take to your lip
A last maidenly sip,
The bloom on your cheek to delay ;
It may make you immortal,
I verily think,
As a fountain of Ink !
I am sure it contains
In its many recesses,—
Though now in solution—
When mixed with your brains,
Full many a stanza
Of verses divine,
Of musical measure
And rhythmical line,
And swift-coming fancies
In verses divine !

But its witchery true
Will be thrown around you
When the birds and the bees

And the winds and the trees,
In a concert of song
The sweet twilight prolong,
And your thoughts wander forth
To your home in the North;
To the mountains and snows
Where the anthracite glows;
To the hearth and the grate,
And the dinner at eight;
To the shelves and the books
In the quaint little nooks;
To the welcoming word
When your footstep was heard,
That greeted you always
At Centre and Third!

March.

I.

FROM the chambers of the North,
March, the stormy, rushes forth,
Hands and arms and body bare,
Fiery eyes and streaming hair,
Roaring out his battle-yell,
Like a demon fierce from hell ;
Riding on the viewless wind,
Which old winter left behind,
Sweeping from the mountain side
Through the ravine far and wide ;
Piling up the blinding snow
Where the winter torrents flow ;
Driving down the biting hail
In a fierce and blust'ring gale ;
While along his wasteful track
Furious blasts the forest wrack,
And beneath him, year by year,
Mountain giants disappear,

Tumbling from the rooted rock,
With a sullen roar and shock,
Adding terror and affright
To the horrors of the night!

II.

Nor upon the solid ground
Is alone the havoc found ;
Raving round the darkened pole
Angry waters rush and roll,
While upon the heaving tide
Icebergs huge and monstrous ride,
And beyond the rocky shore
Comes the maelstrom's fearful roar;
Clouds career athwart the sky,
Moon and stars go scudding by ;
Down the raging main full fast,
Rides he on a mighty blast ;
High he flings the ocean wave,
Sinks her fleets in watery grave,
Sweeps from off the trackless seas
Thousand splendid argosies !

Works of man his playthings are—
Peaceful yacht or ship of war,
Heart of oak and rib of steel,
All his matchless fury feel!

III.

Stormy March! my welcome take!
Spring will follow in thy wake:
Aries now receives the sun
And the winter days are done.
Howsoever hard it blow,
Crocus lances pierce the snow ;
Passion-flowers look golden gay
For the Easter holiday ;
Breaking from its icy chill
Leaps and flows the sparkling rill,
And the merry bluebirds sing
Welcome to the coming spring !
Stormy March! my blessing take !
Spring doth follow in thy wake.

To Margaret.

HAVE thou a care, most trustful Margaret,
Who comes a-wooing to thy garden-gate ;
Keep him a suppliant,
Nor grant a favor thou canst not recall.

It is enough that he in Eden walks,
And the sweet perfume of its shrubs inhales,
Nor let him cross the stream
That keeps the way, 'twixt him and Paradise.

Oft shall he circle the forbidding walls,
Oft seek the breeze that wantoned with thy hair,
Reach for thy absent self,
And think he sees thee though thou be not
there.

Thou, unessayed, art ever fair and pure,
A kiss, a touch, a step may break the charm ;
    Then keep thee to thyself,
        The sought-for gem is ever prized the most.

While thus he stands an humble suppliant,
Thou art the mistress of his fate and thine ;
    Pass but the Rubicon—
        He is the Cæsar, thou the fallen Rome.

Therefore beware, most trustful Margaret,
Who comes a-wooing to thy garden-gate ;
    While ignorance is bliss—
        The Tree of Knowledge grows in Paradise !

On the Mountain.

COME, Love! the year is dying!
  Touched by the frosty breath
    Of Boreas rude ;
  On the hillside are lying
The leaves, that yesterday,
  Clothed the green wood.

The birds are congregating
  With leader and with mate,
    For early flight ;
The stormy clouds are gathering ;
  Soon will the mountain-tops
    Be clothed in white.

Come, ere the birds departing,
  Unpeople all the grove,
    And song be fled ;
And giant winds upstarting,
  Whistle through leafless boughs,
    "The year is dead !"

Stoicisms.

LIFE is short : at every turn
Grows a flowret or a thorn ;
Let us gather while we may
Sweets the Fates will not delay ;
This is wisdom,—who would grieve ?
Sorrow comes to all who live.
Though we through this being toil,
Lost in glory or turmoil,
Let the sorrows of to-day
By to-morrow pass away.
Let the heart be bright and free,
Borrow not of misery.
True, the loved of Heaven die young,
As an ancient poet sung ;
And though memory often rolls
Bygone sorrows o'er our souls,
And some trains of thought bring on
Images of loved ones gone,
Still they quickly pass away,
Like the night before the day,

And that momentary scene
Follows things that long have been.
Were it not that He above
Truly is a God of love ;
Were it not that time can heal
All the sorrows that we feel,
As it to the lip doth press
The golden cup, Forgetfulness,—
So much anguish passes through
Life, with which we have to do,
Ere the work was well begun
We should feel the race was run.
Who would gird him for the strife
Looking backward upon life ?
But the wound of yesterday
Heals before the next affray,
And, forgetful of the smart,
Gird we up, and play our part
With a callousness of heart
Which the world could never guess
Had it known our deep distress.

A Ballad.

 MAIDEN went up to the north coun-
    trie,
        Lingle, lingle, lee ;
She was as pretty as pretty could be,
        Lingle, lingle, lee ;
And she had been there but scarcely a day,
    A day but only three,
Till she stole a poor fellow's heart away,
    O, lingle, lingle, lee.

And he was as sad as sad could be,
    Lingle, lingle, lee,
When the maiden left for the south countrie,
    Lingle, lingle, lee ;
And she had been home but scarcely a day,
    A day but only three,
Till he came for the heart she had stolen away
    O, lingle, lingle, lee.

But she would not give up, as each one could
 see,
   Lingle, lingle, lee,
The heart she had stole from the north countrie,
   Lingle, lingle, lee ;
So they talked it over but scarcely a day,
   A day but only three ;
She gave him her heart and he took it away,
   O, lingle, lingle, lee.

But lately he came from the north countrie,
   Lingle, lingle, lee,
And they were as happy as happy could be,
   Lingle, lingle, lee.
He came with his friends but scarcely a day,
   A day but only three,
And he gave her a ring and he took her away,
   O, lingle, lingle, lee.

Woman.

IN the beginning it was Nature's plan
Woman should be a helpmeet for the
man ;
And some there are who in the toil of
life
Fill well the modest rôle of helpful wife.

But when the woman moral ruin wrought,
Her love she for our consolation brought ;
Consoler, helper, then she was to be,
And bear the yoke with loving sympathy ;
And some there are who in the toil of life
Fill well the rôle of the consoling wife.

From human passion free,—to her the word
Came in due time,—the handmaid of the Lord,—
From her chaste body, faithful, loving, fair,
The great Deliverer came our state to share ;

Children of earth exalted to the skies,
With her brought down, with her again to rise ;
And some there are who in the toil of life
Fill well the rôle of the exalting wife.

Then blessings on her head whose helping hand
Would scatter roses o'er a barren land ;
Bless her who with a loving heart could go
Forth with her spouse where thorns and thistles
    grow ;
Blessings on her who patiently could wait
The slow revolving years to crown her state ;
And though a perfect character is rare,
And few indeed this threefold duty bear,
Yet some there are who in the toil of life
Fill well this model of the perfect wife.

Forgive, then, gentle woman all her faults,—
Thrice blest is she who helps, consoles, exalts.

Ad Evam.

 DO not see among thy sighing train
Of full enamoured youths one weak or
   vain ;
 Though each admirer, dressed with
   greatest care,
With beard well trimmed and curled and bar-
 bered hair,
Virtuous, well read, devoted seems to be,
But yet, dear Eva, scarcely worthy thee.

Thy neat attire, unmarred by flounce or frill,
Thy light brown hair afloat at thy wild will,
Thy sculptured lip, brow neither low nor high,
That beauteous gem, thy calm and clear blue eye,
Tell us full well how fair, how pure thou art,
But do not tell us who shall win thy heart.

Safe at my hands this offering thou may'st take,
For though thy presence does my senses wake,

And oft the matchless beauty of thy charms
The freezing current in my bosom warms,
Old Time my folly does full well betray
And sprinkles through my hair the tell-tale gray;
And yet I would not that it e'er could be
Charms such as thine could have no charms for
  me.

In full-blown beauty 'mid thy bridal band,
With trembling joy I see thee give thy hand,
But do not see what happy man shall sip
The honey from thy chaste and pouting lip:
No fopling, I am sure, shall taste such bliss,—
A generous, whole-souled man should have that
  kiss.

Not e'en to thee has yet appeared, perchance,
The looked-for hero of thy young romance;
But whose soe'er that bliss, I pray thy life
May thenceforth pass, a well-loved, faithful wife.

Wisdom.

HAPPY is he that findeth thee,
Blest is the man doth thee possess!
For better than the merchandise
Of silver from the richest mine,
Or gain of finest gold, thou art.
Thou art to him more precious far
Than choicest pearls or rubies are ;
And all the things he can desire
Compared to thee are nothing worth :
Thou art to him the life of life—
With thee he shall have length of days,
Riches and honors are thy gifts ;
With thee he walks in pleasant ways,
And all his paths are paths of peace.

After the Battle.

'VE trod the slippery path of fame,
  I've burned at honor's story,
I've sought to win myself a name
  On battle-fields of glory ;
Where bright the bristling bayonets rose
  And blood flowed free,
I fiercely have encountered foes,
  For thee, for thee.

Danger and death full oft I've dared,
  Have seen the cannon flashing,
Have rushed, with arm for combat bared,
  Where sabres bright were clashing ;
Then sunk to rest, when day had fled,
  Beneath a tree,
And when in sleep's oblivion dead
  Have dreamed of thee.

How blest the visions !—Hope was then
  In each bright dream she made me ;

Ah! must they never come again?
　　And has dark Fate betrayed me?
Hopeless I wish that thou wert mine,—
　　Say, wilt thou be?
For all my fondest wishes twine
　　Round thee, round thee.

A Serenade.

'TIS midnight hour : the world in sleep
   Is gently borne through empty
      space,
  Whilst I a restless vigil keep,
Still haunted by thy face.
   But, dear one, rest, and dream that we
    Are arm in arm in yonder grove,
  Whilst I am whispering low to thee
  My simple tale of love.

'Tis midnight hour : an angel guard
  Is watching o'er thy chaste repose ;
Oh, make that right my dear reward,
  That care on me impose !
   Rest, dear one, rest, and dream that we
    Are arm in arm in yonder grove,
  Whilst I am whispering low to thee
  My simple tale of love.

'Tis midnight hour : but when the beams
  Of morning ope the eye of day,
Remember in thy early dreams
  The burden of this lay ;
    Sleep, dear one, sleep, and dream that we
      Are arm in arm in yonder grove,
    Whilst I am whispering low to thee
      My simple tale of love.

The Serpent.

A Fragment.

INVOCATION.

IF once again to mortal may appear
Some vision of the morning age sub-
    lime,
    Like that vouchsafed to him, the latest
    seer
Who forward looked adown the gulf of Time,
And saw the Angel from the heavenly sphere,
Bind with a chain the Serpent, old in crime;
Grant me to tell his subtilty and wile
When in the long ago he did the world beguile!

PROEM.

THE beast first named on page of Holy Writ,
Whose ministry was the development

Of what in man was mortal—whose quick wit
Saw the weak point, and in pure devilment,
With tortuous subtle speech went straight for it,
And made for evil the first argument,
Rousing the passions whence our woes all
  . spring—
The wise and subtle Serpent—Him I sing.

He taught our mother Eve one phase of love,
Planted ambition in her lowly mind,
With sweet insinuating accents strove
To make her senses to corruption blind,
Filled her with unbelief of Him above,
To labor and desire the world consigned;
And hence it comes wherever man has trod
Thistles and thorns spring from the accursed
    sod.

That early morn in Paradise the blest,
When for the first essayed to go alone
That paragon of beauty in whose breast
There was no guile and in whose bright eye shone
The fire of love—but lacking the true test
Of love, obedience fond—which might atone,

Excuse, or palliate the sad mistake
Which she committed with that guileful snake:

In that first interview much more was said
And done than has come down to us in speech;
The Serpent must have put a wily head
Upon the woman, else could she o'erreach
The Lords of the Creation? deftly spread
A net-work of sweet smiles over the peach
Of her smooth cheek, and with a single hair
Lead doting manhood with her any where?

Ay, not alone in eating were those hours
Spent by that apple-tree—a world was sold,
Mankind was ruined, and enormous powers
Persuasive, and of witcheries untold
Were granted to her in those odorous bowers,
By which the race is ever since cajoled:—
A solemn league and covenant they made
Each other evermore to help and aid.

Man is as wax beneath her plastic hand,
Age brings no wisdom if a woman sues,
Honor and fame, houses and gold and land
Vanish before her like the early dews;

Her lightest wish is to him a command,
He cannot if he would her suit refuse ;
How came she by that all resistless power ?
From that wise Serpent in that morning hour.

Mountain Musings.

THE long-continuing autumn of the years
    When we were young and wandered
      by the streams,
    And by the woods, sweet smelling,
    Seems to come back no more.

The amber-hued September with its fruits,
Golden or purple, scenting the pure air,
    And to the landscape giving
    Richness and sweet content ;

The soft-eyed cattle, watched by shepherd dog,
Cropping with lazy jaw the aftermath,
    And to the milkmaid lowing
    When sinks the weary sun ;

The rich aroma of the moaning pine,
Of the sweet fern or of the grasses wild,
    On sighing breezes floating
    To feast the grateful sense ;

The music of the quivering forest leaf,
The chirp of bird calling to distant mate,
  The autumn insect humming
    The song of afternoon ;

The chipmunk scampering on the ragged fence,
Or watching by his home on gnarled tree-root,
  He sits with saucy perking
    And jaws with nuts distent ;

—These things are lost to these degenerate days—
These days are short, soon sinks the autumn sun,
  On the horizon hanging
    Clouds, dark with wind and storm !

The air is thick with dust raised by the rush
Of thousand chariots on the public ways,
  Each to be foremost striving,
    To gain some petty end.

From yon dense city rolls the acrid smoke
With lurid flame, from many an iron throat,
  The blessed sun obscuring
    Though at the hour of noon.

The clatter of innumerable mills,
The hurry of innumerable feet
From dark to daylight going,
And then from day to dark—

The babel of innumerable tongues,
The striking of innumerable hands,
The world's rude business making
The first and last of life ;

The rush and roar of fiercely coming train,
The demon scream rebounding on the hills ;—
These are the harsh surroundings
That please this age of gold.

So we escape unto the mountain-top,
And seek the restful silence of the woods,
And with the hills communing
Cast not a thought below.

The Death of Saul.

 SOUND of battle
On Gilboa's hills,
A shout of triumph
In the vale Jezreel ;
Dire sights of slaughter
By the babbling fount,
Dull groans of dying,
Shrieks of agony,
A roar of tempest
And a trampling host :
The shield flung vilely
And the broken spear
Speed the fugitive.

Like a giant oak
When the storm is past
Stands the goodly king,
Saul of the stately head :
Beaten, overcome,
But yet unsubdued !

O great-hearted Saul!
Thy fate hath met thee
In the trembling witch
That brought up Samuel
At the midnight hour
To denounce thy doom,
Thine, thy house, thy sons.

The sound of battle
Lessens on the gale,
Victor and vanquished,
With the heat and strife
Sink in the coming night,
And the weary hand
No more clasps the spear,
No more bears the shield.
The sword, now useless
To defend or strike,
Seeks the heart of Saul!
The armor-bearer
Falls by his master,
And the setting sun
Shows thy trodden banks
Red with Israel's blood,

O ancient river,
Thou river Kishon.

All night long they lay
Upon the silent hill,
Where the fierce battle
Found and overcame
And passed them by.

Now when broke the dawn
Came to strip the slain
The fierce Amalekite,
The mountain robber,
The rude camp follower
Of the Philistine.
The pride of Israel
Lay there cold in death,
Slain by no meaner hand.

And anon they shout
Each to his fellow,
And from camp to camp
Proclaim and publish
The overthrow of Saul;
And soon all the land
Rung with the triumph.

Then his severed head
Forth to Ashdod borne
In Dagon's temple
Fastened, they salute
With cheers derisive.

And his armor bright,
Rudely wrenched from him,
Hang they as a trophy
In the Ashtaroth,
Their idol temple
At far Ashkelon.

To thy walls Beth-shan
His royal body
With his gallant sons,
Now no longer feared,
They hang and fasten.

But the valiant men,
Loyal to thy name,
Arose and took thee
And thy royal sons
From off thy walls, Beth-shan,
And the bodies, burned

At Jabesh, the charred bones
Buried beneath a tree
With lamentations.

O great-hearted Saul!
Thy fate hath met thee
On the field of strife
Braving a kingly death!
But not for thee, death
Stricken in heady fight!

To your tents once more,
O host of Israel,
Till the poet king
Shall sound the high chord
Upon the mountain,
Whose lamenting note
Down the stream of time
Shall forever bear
The name of Saul,
The beauty of Israel,
And his valiant son,
The princely Jonathan,
The ever-faithful friend.

Swifter than eagles,
Stronger than lions,
The bow of Jonathan
And the sword of Saul
Returned not empty
In the day of strife!

Weep! O ye daughters,
Daughters of Israel,
Your dainty delights,
Your silk apparel,
Your scarlet garments,
And your rings of gold!

Gnash your teeth, O sons!
Your spears are broken,
Your shields flung away,
Your swords ungirded:
The Philistines shout
And dwell in your cities,
The heathen triumph
And deride your God.
The daughters of Gath,
The men of Ashkelon

Sing it in their streets,
Shout it together
In the Ashtaroth,
Parade great Dagon
Before Israel.
And in every place
Call to each other,
" Where is now their God ? "

And Israel mourns
Upon the high places,
And puts on sackcloth
And goes warily,
And laments and says
" The God of battles,
The God of Israel,
Hath put by His sword,
It is no longer
Girded upon His thigh !

" The mighty are fallen !
The weapons of war
Are utterly perished ! "

OOR Bessie dead! Now may the
    frightened mice
    Creep from their holes and run about
    at ease,
Nor fear of being picked up in a trice
    By the quick, vigilant, and sleek Maltese.

E'en when she slept one eye was open still,
    And not a mouse could venture to the light
But Bessie knew,—such was her native skill,
    And soon its short career was ended quite.

She was so modest, had such quiet ways,
    Her cry of discontent was never heard;
Stretched at her ease throughout the sunny days,
    Her sup of bread and milk she much preferred.

She was a mouser not from love of blood,—
    'Twas Nature set her 'gainst the rodent tribe;

She scarcely tasted of the dainty food,
    But much enjoyed the torture and the gibe.

But Bessie to the shades herself has passed,—
    Now rests her body 'neath the apple-trees ;
Such quiet as a cat can have at last
    Be ever hers,—my beautiful Maltese !

The Eleventh Psalm.

N the Lord put I my trust—
Say ye then unto my soul
She should flee unto the hill
As a bird by fowler sought?
Let the wicked bend their bow,
Fix the arrow on the string,
From behind the hedges shoot
At His servants, true of heart;—
God the wicked will cast down,
And upon them will He rain
Coals of fire and tempest fierce,—
This shall be their bitter cup.
Seated high upon His throne,
He the righteous will preserve,
For He loveth righteousness
And delighteth in the just!

The Forty-second Psalm.

S the hart longeth for the water brooks,
So my soul longeth after Thee, O God
So my soul thirsteth for the living
God!
My tears have been my meat by day and night
While thus they question—"Where is now thy
God?"
These things will I remember, O my soul!
How with the multitude I passed along,
How with the voice of joy and praise, I went
Into thy house, and there kept holy day.
Why then, my soul, art thou disquieted?
Why art thou so cast down—wait thou for God—
For yet His presence shall give plenteous help:
Deep calleth unto deep with dreadful noise,
Thy waves and billows are gone over me:
Yet will His song be with me in the night,
His loving-kindness bless me every day,
And from mine enemies be my defence.

Why then art thou disquieted, my soul ?
Why art thou so cast down—hope thou in God—
For I shall praise Him yet who is my health,
My countenance, my rock against my foes.

The One Hundred and Second Psalm.

HIDE not thy face in troublous times,
Incline thine ear unto my call,
For now my bones burn on the hearth,
And all my days consume in smoke.
Now is the void and trackless waste
The habitation of my soul;
For I am like the pelican,
Alone within the wilderness;
Or like the solitary owl
That sits within the desert vast:
I sleep not, but am desolate,
And like a sparrow on the house,
I watch alone through weary hours.

The One Hundred and Third Psalm.

THE days of man are but as grass,
His life as flowers of the field,
His body as the fleeting dust,
Or like a shadow in the hills.
But thou, O Lord, shalt still abide:
For though the earth shall pass away,
The heavens and all their shining host;
Thou through all ages art the same,
And of thy years shall be no end.

The Fifth Ode.

WHAT silly boy perfumed with liquid
    unguents,
   Within thy sweet retreat, 'mid many
    roses,
  Urges his suit, O Pyrrha!
  For whom dost dress thy yellow hair
So simply beautiful? Oft, alas! thy faith
And changing gods unkind shall he bemoan,
  And gaze in wonder on the seas
  Rough with black winds tempestuous,
Who now enjoys thee, thinking thee all golden,
And always gay, with welcome to his wooing
  Hopes thee—change unsuspecting.
  O most unhappy are those youths
To whom thou, unessayed, art fair. But for me,
The sacred wall, by votive tablet, shows my robes
  Still dripping, there suspended
  To the powerful God of Sea.

Hadrian, ad Animulam.

Animula, vagula, blandula,
Hospes, comesque corporis,
Quæ nunc abibis, in loca
Pallidula, rigida, nudula,
Nec ut soles, dabis jocos.

THOU little, wandering, courteous
    sprite,
Friend and companion of my heart,
Where wouldst thou now from me
    depart?
Thou pale and wan and naked art,
And canst no more to mirth incite!

———

Life of my life! Thou dear eluding sprite
Whose courteous presence ever gave delight,
Guest and companion dear hast thou become,
And mad'st, these many years, myself thy home:
Part we now? Whither wouldst thou hie, my
    Life,
Pale, stately, and exposed? Where wilt thou find

234

Companionship and guide the pleasant strife?
Perchance refused as either friend or guest,
To fate unused and silence thus consigned,
Where then thy gibe, thy mirth-provoking jest?

ECCLESIASTES.

Writers upon the plan and purpose of this book do not agree in their theory, and some go so far as to doubt if there were any special object in the mind of the author. There are those who maintain that it is a mere compilation, like the Book of Proverbs, of maxims and reflections ; others insist that it is a finished work with a definite object, and having four capital divisions of subjects. By some the whole book is held to be a monologue, by others to be a didactic poem, and by still others that it was delivered as a public discourse. Whatever be the fact as between these theories, some of it was written in Hebrew verse and some of it in prose, and it does not seem possible that it ever was, or was intended to be, delivered as a discourse, lecture, or address.

Its religious teaching, in so far as it has any, is a somewhat modified and refined heathen philosophy, and it has been noticed that the word therein translated God is '' Elohim '' in the original, a name applied equally to the true and to false gods. Whether Solomon be the author or compiler, or both or neither, whether the book was written in his age or later, has been denied and asserted, and neither point is any nearer a solution by all which has been written.

Owing to the reprehensible practice of cutting it up into chapters and verses, instead of dividing it by subject and paragraph, the book cannot be read with solid comfort in our ordinary Bible, known as the Authorized Version. But indeed, apart from this mere arbitrary division, scarcely any two scholars or commentators divide the book into exactly the same sections and subjects; and this diversity of opinion among competent scholars is a main and powerful reason for believing that it is a compilation, or perhaps the fragments of, or materials for, a larger work. The same idea occurs again and again, and in language quite similar. To at least five headings, divisions, or subjects, but at irregular intervals, we have the same ending—" There is nothing better for a man than that he should eat and drink, and that he should make his soul enjoy good in his labor "—and which thus seems to have been intended to mark or be the refrain of different portions, in the same manner, perhaps, as the last two verses give us " the conclusion of the whole matter."

But these divisions and conclusions are not introduced and constructed with that finish and symmetry which we have a right to expect in the completed work of so experienced a writer as Solomon. Compared with the exquisite polish of the Song of Songs it does not show the mastery of the practised writer, or the happiness of illustration with which that is filled. The Song of Songs is an exquisite pastoral, one of a thousand and five by the same prolific writer; and although the nature of the matters treated in the Ecclesiastes was not capable of such full poetic description, yet there is very satisfactory reason for concluding that the Book of Ecclesiastes is an incomplete work by King Solomon. Satiety of all earthly enjoyments, a knowledge that all greatness was vanity and riches vexation of spirit, that the strivings of mankind for the greatest good were, after all, mere feeding on wind, that life itself was a burden and death a release from toil and poverty and oppression, mark the thought, experience, and position of the writer, and contain so much of human interest that the book in which these facts, reflections, and conclusions are written will never lose its attraction for the race of man.

The fragmentary character of the work makes it convenient to render it into short odes or lyrics ; and no elaborate treatment of the book as a complete poem has been attempted. The considerable portions which partake largely of the characteristics of the Book of Proverbs, and being in the whole about fifty verses, remain untouched.

Vanity of Labor.

ECCLESIASTES i. 1–12.

HOW vain the work that man hath done,
Or may do, underneath the sun;
  What profit for his toil and care?
His fathers came and passed away,
And he shall have no longer stay.

The sun upon the eastern shore
Ariseth as he rose of yore,
  And goeth down, we know not where;
Yet hasteth eager to his place,
Unwearied in the ceaseless race.

The South wind fans the tasselled grain,
Then, veering to the North amain,
  Blows fiercely from the snow-clad hills,
And veering still on restless wings,
Once more a balmy zephyr brings.

The eye, although it ever see,
The ear, though hearing constantly,
  Nor sound nor sight to surfeit fills ;
Nor can great rivers flowing free
Make full the all-receiving sea.

Is there a thing, whereof men say
Lo, this is new ! I tell you nay,
  What hath been, that again shall be.
What done, that shall again be done,
And nothing new shall see the sun.

Forgotten are the former things,
The names of heroes and of kings,
  And comes the evil day when we
Shall be unknown,—but why deplore ?
The earth abideth evermore.

Vanity of Wisdom.

 SOUGHT for wisdom with a constant
heart,
And to know all that under heaven
is done,
Which travail sore God giveth every son
Of man, of his afflicted lot, as part.
And I have seen all works beneath the sun,
And lo! I found them to be vanity;
That which is crooked, crooked shall remain,
What is defective, still defective be,—
So much to know is so much vanity.

I that was king within Jerusalem,
And gat me wisdom more than all of them
Which sat before me in that kingly place,
And much experience had in ways of men,
In wisdom, and in knowledge of the world,
Spake to my heart, and with it thus communed:

"O heart!" I said, "behold thy great estate!
Through thy much wisdom be not thou elate;
Thou knowest madness, folly thou dost know,
And the vain hopes that with this knowledge go:
 Why search out wisdom? she gives no
  relief,—
Who hath much wisdom he too hath much grief;
Increase of knowledge much increaseth pain,—
Thy hopes, thy wishes, O my heart, are vain!"

Vanity of Pleasure.

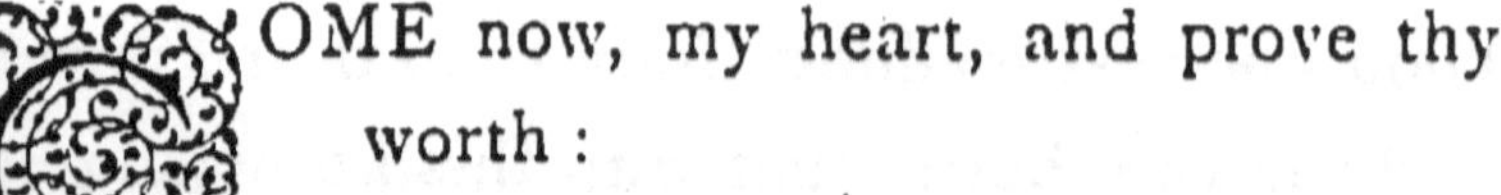

COME now, my heart, and prove thy
worth :
Let every pleasure have its birth,
Call madding laughter to thy side,
Let mirth her boisterous courses ride ;
Give thyself up to cheerful wine,
Nor wisdom's guidance quite resign ;
Lay hold on folly till thou see
What the chief good of man may be,
Which he should seek in toil and strife
For all his days of mortal life :—
What, O my heart ! what dost thou see ?
Vexation all and vanity !

Go, make great works : build houses fine,
Make gardens, orchards ; plant the vine,
And lead from the surrounding hills
To glassy pools the sparkling rills,

To court the balmy evening breeze
And irrigate thy fruitful trees ;
Get servants for thy growing state,
And herds and cattle, small and great ;
Gather the silver and the gold,
Hoard for thy pleasure sums untold,—
Get for thy house those precious things
That grace the palaces of kings ;
Let music's daughters round thee throng
With mirth and wine, and dance and song,
Viol and harp, and every sort
Of instrument of joy and sport ;
Let there be no unfilled desire
For all thy heart may yet require,
Keep not thyself from any joy,
In pleasure all thy time employ ;
This is the wages thou hast won
By all thy labor 'neath the sun :—
    What, O my heart ! what dost thou see ?
Vexation all and vanity !

    See in the midst fair wisdom stand,
Madness and folly on each hand ;
As light the darkness doth excel,

So wisdom folly.   Mark them well !
The wise man's eyes are in his head,
The fool doth in the darkness tread,
And yet the same event doth fall
To fool and wise, to one and all :
Inquire and find wherein, then, lies
Advantage to the fool or wise.
Each seeks, at last, the burial urn
And is forgotten in his turn ;
For each there is the self-same rule,—
As dies the wise so dies the fool :
Consider life, and what is done
By fool and wise beneath the sun,—
Whose works shall stand, whose name shall thrill
The coming man in good or ill ?
None shall survive the fleeing day,
Their names, their works shall pass away :—
    What, O my heart ! what dost thou see ?
Vexation all and vanity !

    Mark how thy days are hastening
Thy labors to an end to bring ;
Thy houses grand, thy vineyards green,
No fairer have been ever seen ;

The glassy pools, the gurgling rills,
Fed by the everlasting hills ;
Thy orchards fair with fruitage crowned,
Thy gardens scenting all the ground,
Thy servants, men and maidens fair,
Thy flocks and herds of beauty rare ;
Go to the man, whoe'er he be,
Who in due time shall follow thee :
Thy wisdom great, thy labor sore,
For him have riches laid in store ;
He over all thy works shall rule,
Be he a wise man or a fool :
Despair of all thy labor done
With judgment underneath the sun ;
The toil of many weary years,
Of daily hopes and nightly fears,
Goes in the end, thyself forgot,
The prize of him who labored not :—
    What, O my heart ! what dost thou see ?
Vexation all and vanity !

    If pleasure bring us no relief,
If riches multiply our grief,
If wisdom give no certain light

By which to ward the coming night,
If wise and foolish, to one end,
In undistinguished masses tend,
If all our names forgotten be,
Our knowledge and our equity,
Then there is nothing better than
That both the wise and foolish man
Should eat and drink, and give his soul
Enjoyment in the flowing bowl,
In all the labor of his hands,
In all the product of his lands,
And give his senses joy to know
What good the hands of God bestow
On him who placeth his delight
In faithful words and works of right,
Whereas the sinner may travail
And heap up goods,—to what avail ?
They shall be taken and bestowed
On him whose heart is right with God :—
   Yet, O my heart ! what dost thou see ?
Vexation all and vanity !

Instability of Things.

ACH action hath its season,
　　Each purpose hath its time,—
The spring-time for the planting,
　　The fall to pluck the vine.
The young are ever joying,
　　Or whirling in the dance,
They have no thought of mourning
　　Or fears of dull mischance ;
The lover is embracing
　　The chosen of his heart,
And hours of sweet communing
　　Increase the pain to part ;
The soldier seeks the battle,
　　And frowns at thoughts of peace,
And joys not in the prospect
　　That bloody wars shall cease ;

The youth to age is growing,
  The new to dull and gray,
The fashion of the summer
  The autumn casts away.

And thus all things are changing
  With each returning sun :
What profit in his labor
  Hath he whose work is done ?
A moment it remaineth,
  Then is decay begun !

So, be each man rejoicing,
  To share the good of life,
Be eating and be drinking,
  And shunning care and strife.
The times are ever changing,
  Man's work is ever new,—
What he hath done aforetime,
  That he again shall do.

But whatsoe'er God doeth,
  It shall forever stay ;
To His work no man addeth,
  Nor taketh aught away.

God the Judge.

ECCLESIASTES iii. 16–22.

 SAW the place where judgment sat en-
    throned
And held the scales of justice ; and be-
    hold !
Clothed in the garb of state sate wickedness ;
I turned me to the place of righteousness,
And in those sacred precincts ministered,
In priestly garments, foul iniquity !

Where shall the wicked man stern justice find,
The righteous seek for comfort to his soul ?
All have forsaken justice, mercy, truth !
And then I said, " Lo ! God shall judge the
    world :
The righteous and the wicked all shall stand
Before His place of judgment,—He shall mete
To every man, of all the sons of men,
For every purpose and for every work !"

But who can tell if that the sons of men
Are better than the beasts? to each of them
One thing befalleth.   Death o'ertakes them all,
And man hath no advantage of the beast :
Unto one place they go,—from dust they are,
And unto dust shall each again return !
And if the spirit of the sons of men
Ascendeth, or the spirit of the beast
Descendeth, who can tell?   God knoweth all.

So let each man in his own works rejoice,
And take his portion with a quiet mind,
For who shall bring him back to see or know
What work or change shall happen after him ?

Oppressions.

WHO beareth rule in earthly place
  Hath need of more than earthly grace ;
  For with the rule oppressions grow,
    Whose wrongs bear heavy on the low.
Unused to stand before the king,
Who shall their grievance to him bring ?
For them no champion appears,
Their plea is poverty and tears !
See, lust and rapine rule the hour,
Protected by the hand of power,
Which makes the bold oppressor sure
He may, unchecked, despoil the poor.
The while they groan in pain and toil,
And tend the flocks and till the soil,
Both sons and daughters multiply
And but increase the misery ;
Mere clods of earth, as erst they were,
To whom there comes no Comforter !

The labor that a man hath done,—
His righteous work beneath the sun,
The riches that have blest his hand,
The honor which he may command,
The learning he with toil hath got,
The children crowning all his lot,—
Do in his neighbor gender hate
And envy of his fair estate ;
So that his life of travail sore,
And all his work bring joy no more.

Ay, better is the crust of bread
With quiet, than the ox, stall-fed,
With travail and vexation dread!
And better is a poor wise child
Than an old foolish king, beguiled
Of power, whose weakening reign
No longer can the base restrain,
While more and more oppressions grow
That bear to earth the poor and low,
Whose sighs and groans no one shall hear,—
To whom time brings no Comforter.
"Is life worth living then ?" I said :
"Nay, rather place me with the dead ;

Or better still it were to be
With those, unborn, who may not see
The evil work now daily done
Beneath the all-observing sun."

ECCLESIASTES v. 1-18.

WHEN thy foot goeth to the house of
       God,
       Then give thine ear,
Nor like the fool accept the teach-
  er's rod,—
       Both do and hear ;

Not rash in speech, nor with unseemly mirth,
       Both hear and do ;
God is in heaven and thou upon the earth,—
       Be thy words few.

When thou to Him hast bound thyself by vow,
       See that thou pay :
He hath no love for fools,—thou shouldst not
  vow
       Except thou pay.

Mark that thy mouth cause not thy flesh to sin,
Neither say thou,
Before the angel whose ward thou hast been,
"I did not vow!"

Wherefore should God be angry at thy voice
And raise the rod?
Let fools who have no fear in speech rejoice,
But fear thou God!

To a Miser.

Ecclesiastes v. 9–14.

SET not your heart on shining gold,
For though you reach to sums untold
You'll seek for more!
"Enough?"—it is an empty sound!
Abundance must still more abound,
Enlarge the store;

Then feast your eyes on growing wealth,
Go to your hoarded heaps by stealth
At midnight deep;
Go count your thousands one by one,—
By sheer abundance all undone
You cannot sleep,

Lest watchful death on earthly round
Should seize you while in slumber bound,
Your gold all left;

Or some bold robber should invade
The chamber where your heart is laid,
  Intent on theft.

But yonder laboring man behold
Go to his work in heat and cold
  At rising sun ;
And watch him as he nightly goes
To sound and undisturbed repose,
  His labor done.

No fear his steady footstep shows,
Nor death nor robbers are his foes,
  Though ever nigh ;
Scatter your gold by noble stealth,
And place your heart, your hopes, your wealth,
  Secure on high.

Wealth Unenjoyed.

ECCLESIASTES vi.

THOUGH God give honor, riches, wealth,
And all that heart of man desires,
Yet if He doth at last withhold
The power to make enjoyment full,
And turneth to a stranger what
Successful toil and care had got,
Then that man's life is vanity.

Though he should live for many years,
An hundred children should beget,
Yet lack fruition of his life ;
Be in his growing age unblest,
Unhonored by his children's love,
Then to the dogs for burial cast,—
Untimely birth would better be.

Who cometh thus in vanity
And goeth in the darkness forth,

Unknown forever by a name,
Unseeing the all-seeing sun,
Of all unknown and knowing naught,
Shall rest in greater quietude
Than he with age and wealth endued.

There is no good in many years,
For all the labor of a man
Is but to gratify his taste,—
Yet is his mouth unsatisfied :
The wisdom of the wise shall be
Just like the folly of the fool,
And both shall end in vanity !

Better the sight of choosing eyes
Than wandering after blind desire,—
But all these things are vanities,
And strivings after vain applause :
Like to a shadow in the prime
Man passeth, and shall never know
What things shall be in after time.

The Two Houses.

ET us go where the mourners as-
    semble,
  And not to the house of the feast ;
    For our sorrow is better than
    laughter,
  And sadness improveth the heart.

In the house where the mourners assemble
  The dead shall a lesson impart,
The living shall look on his ending,
  The living shall lay it to heart.

To the house where the mourners assemble,
  The heart of the wise goeth forth,
But the fool, with his laughter and singing,
  Regardeth the mansion of mirth.

Let us hear the rebuke of a wise man,
  Nor list to the voice of the fool,
For his laugh is like thorns in the burning,
  And vanity filleth his song.

Corruptions.

SEE how oppression beareth down
The needy poor beneath his frown ;
Where'er he treads no pleasures spring,
No flowers bloom, no children sing.
Though industry with daily toil
May tend the flock and till the soil,
And gather, ere the latter rain,
The fatted kine, the golden grain,
The lord alone shall taste the feast,—
The hind may huddle with the beast.
   Surely the wise man in his wrath
Will sweep oppression from his path,—
Raise up the weak, beat down the strong,
Establish justice, banish wrong,
Be leader in the righteous cause
Of brotherhood and equal laws !
   But scarcely is the work begun
Until the people's champion

Is called to counsel with the king,
And state his cause for murmuring :
  Then see him coming to their aid,
In gold and purple silks arrayed,
On steed, with trappings richly dight,
And sword and shield of dazzling light,
With softened voice and weakened zeal
Protesting for the commonweal !

  Where is that clear resounding voice
Which made the populace rejoice ?
Where is the sympathetic eye
Whose glances like the lightning fly ?
Why is the wise young leader calm ?—
A gift hath touched his itching palm !
  Blind are his eyes, corrupt his heart,
Unequal to the glorious part;
By sugared promises controlled,
And the soft blandishment of gold !
The work but late so well begun
Hath reached its end, although undone.
  Ah ! more than wisdom is required
By him with hate of wrong inspired;
An honest heart, a love of right

For its own self, will give him might;
But more than all, in him must reign
A holy scorn of sordid gain!
  Then ask the cause why former days
Were worthy of the poet's praise;
Ask why the poor man's life should be
Vexation, toil, and vanity;
Why lute and song should now no more
Call laughing childhood to the fore;
Ask why the maid should go unwed,
And age in rags and sorrow tread?
  And when the spirit rises high,
Well may the anger-speaking eye
Strike terror to the proud and fool,
For law and right again shall rule!
  And when the end is fairly won,
By honest work with patience done;
Then shall we say beneath the sun,
"Well ended what was well begun!"

ECCLESIASTES vii. 11–22.

ISDOM is better than gold inherited.
It is a profit to them that see the sun.
For though wisdom defends from ad-
versity,
And money may also be a sure defence;
Yet knowledge is more excellent than gold,
For wisdom giveth life to them that have it.
If thou wilt consider then the ways of God,
That which is awry shall not be made straight,
For the works of God remain as at the first.

In the day of thy prosperity be joyful;
In the day of thine adversity consider;
For God hath made the one ever to remain
A set-off over and against the other.
In the days of my vain life have I seen much:
A just man perisheth in his righteousness,
A wicked prolongeth his life in wickedness.

Be not righteous overmuch, neither too wise ;
Be not overmuch wicked, neither foolish,
Lest thou be desolate or die before thy time.
He that feareth God shall come forth of them all.
In wisdom is more strength than in ten mighty
    men.

Because no man doeth good and no sin,
Take not heed of all the words that are spoken ;
Perchance thou mayest hear thy servant curse
    thee ;
Reflect, then, that thou thyself hast cursed
    others.

Against Woman.

ECCLESIASTES vii. 23–29.

 SAID I will be wise, and know
The secret springs of joy and woe ;
But when I strove the cause to find,
Unfathomed was the Eternal Mind ;
Far in the past was what I sought,
Deep, deep beyond my reach of thought :
And yet my heart was set to know
And seek for wisdom, and search out
The reason and the course of things ;—
Full soon I found that wickedness
Is foolishness and madness dire,
But when the question mounted higher,—
Why man, created upright, fell,
Or seized occasion to rebel,
Disdaining laws that sought to bind
The action of the aspiring mind ;
Why growth of evil was allowed,
Why goodness shrinks within the crowd,

Why light and life and love are dear,
Why friendship gives a joy sincere,
Why death is such a bitter foe?
All this I sought but could not know.
    And still, beyond this search of things,
Which but half knowledge with it brings,
It came within my settled plan
To search and find a loyal man,—
One in the hour of wisdom true,
And in the hour of folly too;
True in the high, exulting hour
When youth gives permanence to power,—
True when the days of failing age
Require support and counsel sage:
And in that search this world around,
One in a thousand have I found
From whom my soul would not depart,—
A faithful, honest, loyal heart.
    But in my search I did not find
One woman with a candid mind,—
One with a heart from selfhood free,
One not enslaved by vanity.
Gewgaws and gold engross their cares,
Their subtle hearts are nets and snares,

Caresses by their soft white hands
Bind you as if with iron bands;
Beware of all their wanton wiles,
And be not drunken with their smiles;
Than death more bitter was the thought
Of so much harm by woman wrought,
And that in all the world around
Not one trustworthy could be found!

Respect to Kings.

WHO, as the wise man, stands before
    the king
  And knows to shape his words in
    grave debate ?
The wise man who, with shining face sedate,
Gives in due speech the meaning of the thing ?
He grave obedience to the king doth bring,
  And in God's fear allegiance to the state ;
  Unquestioning his word obeyeth straight,
Knowing the power it beareth from the king.
He who doth thus obey shall never feel
  The shadow of the shade of cold neglect ;
    And the wise man doth know within his heart
That whatsoever wrong time may reveal,
  God in His course, whatever men reflect,
    Shall well correct and even every part.

Providence Over All.

ECCLESIASTES viii. 6-11.

GOD'S rule is over all to work His will,
  And even kings are subject to His
      sway;
  He giveth time and judgment in His
      course,
And all their chosen plans are brought to nought
And their proud labors hasten to decay;
Who then dare plan against His sure decree,—
Whose purpose shall succeed, whose purpose
    fail?
None among all the sons of men can know
What shall be, or what moment may bring forth
Event untoward to his whole design.

Even his own spirit lies beyond his power,
And mortal man shall not prolong his life
Nor have control over his day of death;
That day shall come as surely as the sun,—

That final struggle must be met and made ;
It cometh to the wicked and the good,
And from that war there shall be no discharge !

All this I saw when as I gave my heart
To know the secrets of this busy life,
And contemplate the acts of busy men,
And every labor done beneath the sun.

Vain is the wish for any earthly fame,
Oblivion hides the glory and the shame :
Feel not secure to live in coming time,
For I have seen the wicked and the good
Go to the grave, each from his proper place,
And in their city soon forgotten quite.

However long may seem the law's delay,
At last will come the fatal judgment day.

Because the sentence against evil work
And execution of the judgment sealed
Come not with speed upon the sinner's head,
Therefore he saith, " God doth it not remark,"
Till vengeful justice strikes the doubter dead !

Eat and Drink.

THOUGH a sinner do evil an hundred
    times,
    And his days be prolonged,
    Yet surely I know that the end shall
    be well
With all them that fear God ;
But it shall not be well with the wicked,
    Nor his days be prolonged,—
His days which are only a shadow,—because
    He feared not before God.

And yet, when I see that the just man fares
    As the wicked doth fare,
And the wicked are blest in their doings
    As the righteous should be,
And the world still goes in its constant course
    All unmindful of this,—
Then of life and of time and of judgment dread
    I am forced to despair ;

And I find not on earth that full justice done
    Which the wicked require,
And I mourn as I see them exult them
    O'er our travail and toil,
And I feel that the wicked are jeering
    At our labors so vain.

———

And then I said, "Come forth, you minstrel
        throng,
    And lead your sister Mirth ;
The happy days, the pleasant nights prolong :
    Why should the smiling earth,
Which carols to the kissing sun a song,
    Witness of joy a dearth ?
Tell me, where is there any better thing
    Under the glowing sun
Than just to eat and drink, to dance and sing,—
    Our daily labor done,—
And seize enjoyment in the passing day
    Which God in kindness gave,
That of man's labor shall abide alway
    Until he seek the grave ?"

God Over All.

ECCLESIASTES viii. 16–17 ; ix. 1–6.

WHEN I applied my heart to know
And see the business done on earth,
I saw it was the work of God ;
Nor can man find the labor done,
Although he seek, beneath the sun.

For I considered in my heart,
That whether of the righteous man
Or of the wise, all of their work
Is in the hand of God, and He
Keeps all things in obscurity.

And all things come alike to all,—
The righteous and the wicked man,
The good, the unclean and the clean ;
And ever-conquering death comes both
To him who makes or fears an oath.

Yet to the living there is hope :
A living dog is better far
Than is the noblest lion dead ;
The living know that they shall die,
The dead, unknowing all things, lie.

Their love no longer stirs the heart,
Their hatred now is perished quite,
No active zeal their envy wakes ;
Nothing they know of what is done
By living men beneath the sun.

To a Young Man.

ECCLESIASTES ix. 7-10; xi. 9-10.

REJOICE, O young man, in thy youth,
  And walk in the ways of thy heart,
    In the sight of thine eyes;
  Give sorrow no place in thy breast,
Put penance away from thy flesh,
  And the wise men despise.

Sit down to the banquet with joy,
And drink thy heart merry with wine;
  Let thy garments be white,—
Thy head with sweet unguents anoint,
And live whilst thou livest this life :—
  Do thy work with thy might!

But know thou the work which thou doest,
Thy joy in the sun and his light,
  In the feast and the wine,

Shall show as the folly of fools
When wise men shall meet to consult
    Of this labor of thine.

How, then, when the sun shall grow dark
And cometh the Ancient of Days
    To the work of thy hands?
The wood and the stubble and straw
Shall consume, and nothing be left
    Of thy house on the sands.

Contradictions.

O with thy might whate'er thy hand
shall find ;
Nor leave undone the purpose of thy
life ;
There is no work, there is no sage device,
Nor knowledge that shall bring thee a release,
Nor wisdom that shall aid thee to escape
From the dark grave to which thou art consigned !
And yet, I find that in this laboring life,
The swift is not the victor in the race,
The wage of battle goes not to the strong,
The wise man is obliged to beg his bread,
And men of understanding get not wealth :
The charlatan secures the giddy crowd,
While men of skill and merit have no place !
Subject to time and chance, the spreading sail
May catch or fail to catch a favoring gale,
For man, however wise, knows not the time

To tempt the wave and seek the happier clime ;
Though smooth the deep, at once the billows war,
And the frail bark is hurried from the shore,
And winds and waves in elemental strife,
In evil time destroy the laboring life
With sudden stroke, and caught thus unaware,
No hand shall loose him from the fatal snare !

Wisdom Unappreciated.

A LITTLE city stood,
      The pride of all the plain,
  Few men within its walls
      Its honor to maintain ;
And came a mighty king
  And compassed it around,
And heavy bulwarks built
  To raze it to the ground.

The city, in its strait,
  Called to the poor and wise,
And quickly from its gate
  The baffled army flies ;
And when he rose to fame
Forgotten was the name
  Of this poor man and wise,
And none knew whence he came.

Wisdom is more than strength
  Or weapons in the fight,
Yet are its words despised
  When folly stands in sight ;
But when the work is done
Wisdom exalts her son,—
  Her son without a name,
  Her son unknown to fame.

Cautions.

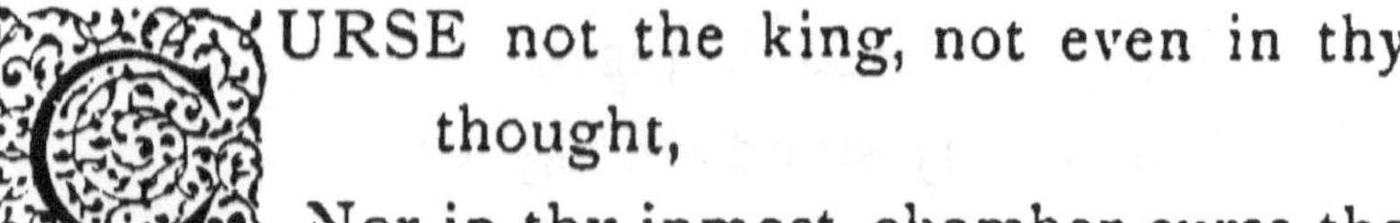

CURSE not the king, not even in thy
 thought,
 Nor in thy inmost chamber curse the
 rich ;
A bird shall bear the echo of thy voice,
And conscience tell the evil thou has wrought.
Upon the waters cast thou forth thy bread,
And thou shalt find it after many days :
Divide to seven, and even unto eight,—
Thou knowest not what evil days may come.
As the full clouds drop rain upon the earth,
Whence thou shalt gather at the harvest-time ;
As the tree falleth to the south or north,
In that place where it falleth it shall be,
So where thy bounty has been well dispensed,
There at thy need it now shall succor thee.
Wait not to sow until the wind be fair,

Lest when the harvest comes thou mayest not
    reap ;
Few things thou knowest, but this shouldst thou
    know,
Whate'er betide, "God's hand is over all :"
Then when the morning cometh sow thy seed,
At evening time withhold not thou thy hand ;
Thou canst not know which may be fully blest,
Or whether both shall not be good alike.

Old Age.

ECCLESIASTES xi. 7–10 ; xii. 1–8.

SWEET is the light to youthful eyes,
  A pleasant thing to see the sun,
But if a man live many years,
  And joys through all their changes
    run,
Let him remember there must be
  Days full of darkness and of fears,
And all be days of vanity.

Then in thy youth rejoice, young man,
  And give thy heart to cheerful days;
Walk in the sight of thy young eyes,
  And follow out the pleasant ways:
But know thou that for every thing
God will thee into judgment bring;
Therefore remove from out thy heart
All that which sorrow may impart;
Let in thy flesh no evil be,—
Manhood and youth are vanity.

And in these days of giddy youth
　Keep thy Creator in thy mind !—
Before the evil days have come,—
Before the carking years draw nigh,
When thou shalt say in wearied tone,
　They bring no pleasure in their train,—
Before the gladsome light grows dark,
　Or clouds return upon the rain :—

Before the keepers of the house
Shall tremble, and the strong man bow
Himself beneath the weight of years,
And teeth shall fail, and sight grow dim,
And doors be shut upon the streets,
And wakeful eyes shall rouse from sleep
At chirping voice of early bird ;

And even Music, maid of mirth,
Shall wail and bow herself to earth ;—
When thou shalt fear the proud and high,
And shrink before the lengthened way,
And dread the terrors in the path ;—
Before the hair shall whitened grow,
And like the almond blossom show,

And daintiest food shall pall the taste,
Which nothing now can stimulate ;—

Before the silver cord be loosed,
Or broken be the golden bowl ;
Before the pitcher at the fount,
Or at the cistern deep the wheel
Be broken—
     And dark Sheol dread
Hides from the sun thy pallid head,
And thou to thy long home art borne,
And mourners go about the streets,
And dust unto the dust return !

ECCLESIASTES xii. 8–14.

THUS the wise-king preacher taught,
Pouring forth digested thought,
And the people sought to know
What his wisdom could bestow.
Gathering up, he set in store
Proverbs from the common lore,
And with his delightsome words
Bound his hearers as with cords;
Words of wisdom, words of truth,
As a goad to urge the youth,
As a nail to fasten well
What the preacher had to tell;
By these words, my son, be led,
By them be admonishéd.

He had seen beneath the sun
What the hands of men had done;
He had mingled with the great,
He had seen their proud estate,

All their troubles, all their cheer,
Day by day, and year by year;
And he knew their life to be
Vexation all and vanity.

He had knowledge, in his rule,
Of the wise and of the fool;
Oft had wearied of discourse
Urged with ever-weakening force;
Listened oft to grave debate
On profound affairs of state;
Many a learnéd treatise read,
Tortured with an aching head;
Given oft, by midnight oil,
Many hours of studious toil,
Till much wisdom seemed to be
Vexation all and vanity.

In his life's protracted round
Here and there a man he found
Who, with true and loyal heart,
Bore his ever-faithful part;
But no woman did he find
With a constant heart and mind :—

Ever changing, insincere,
Ready with a smile or tear ;
Seeking ever for control,
Giving for it self and soul ;
Bartering love for place and pelf,
True to no one but herself ;
Kisses given over night
All forgot by morning light ;
Vows of truth all broken through
Unless power kept them true :
Vows were only empty breath,—
Thought more bitter far than death !—
He had found their vows to be
Vexation, snares, and vanity.

Wisdom wishes to be heard,
Sages hope themselves preferred,
Statesmen full of ancient lore
Con wise maxims o'er and o'er ;
Poets seek the public ear,
Singing words of love and cheer ;—
See what many books abound,
Mostly false, and useless found ;
Not with wine of wit distilled,

But with repetitions filled ;
Stale and stupid, saying o'er
Things much better said before ;
And if even new and fresh,
Wearisome unto the flesh.

What is the conclusion, then,—
The duty of the sons of men ?
What is the supreme command,
Given from the preacher's hand,
That each man may bear away ?

" Fear thou God and Him obey ! "

For He will in open day
Every work to judgment bring,—
Open every secret thing
Good or evil though it be,
Wise or filled with vanity !

TABLE OF FIRST LINES.